Seamus

By

Ronna M. Bacon

Deuteronomy 31:6 Be strong and of a good courage, fear not, nor be afraid of them: for the LORD your God, he it is that does go with you; he will not fail you, nor forsake you.

Psalm 9:9-10 The LORD also will be a refuge for the oppressed, a refuge in times of trouble. And they that know your name will put their trust in you: for you, LORD, have not forsaken them that seek you.

Table of Contents

Chapter 1
Chapter 2
Chapter 3
Chapter 4
Chapter 5
Chapter 6
Chapter 7
Chapter 8
Chapter 9
Chapter 10
Chapter 11
Chapter 12
Chapter 13
Chapter 14
Chapter 15
Chapter 16
Chapter 17
Chapter 18
Chapter 19
Chapter 20
Chapter 21
Chapter 22
Chapter 23
Chapter 24
Chapter 25
Chapter 26
Chapter 27
Chapter 28
Chapter 29
Chapter 30
Chapter 31

Chapter 32
Chapter 33
Chapter 34
Chapter 35
Chapter 36
Chapter 37
Chapter 38
Chapter 39
Chapter 40
Chapter 41
Chapter 42
Chapter 43
Chapter 44
Chapter 45
Chapter 46
Epilogue
Dear Readers

Chapter 1

The air had the scent of late summer, early autumn. The sun hung low in the western sky, shooting out pink and purple rays as it reluctantly sank towards the horizon, reluctant to leave and let the twilight move in. The critters that moved during the day were heading for their rest, leaving the night critters to appear.

Seamus Sloane shut the door on the trailer that held his lawncare equipment. His hand rested on the door for a moment, his eyes raising to the sky. He was exhausted, more exhausted for some reason. It was a Friday night and he had no plans for the weekend, other than to catch up on his own chores. He shook his head before his head bowed and he began to pray, a habit that he had at the end of the day, praying for his staff and then the home owners that were his clients.

Turning, he headed for his truck, his hand resting on the door handle. Seamus turned his head for a moment, a frown crossing his face. The end of day stubble felt rough under his hand as he rubbed at his face, his deep gray eyes thoughtful as he stared around. He felt watched, the sensation increasing over the day. A chime from his phone brought Seamus' attention to that. His sister, Silver, had sent a text message, just asking if they could meet for a meal next week. He smiled. Silver was happily married to Sorley, despite having faced life and death during what they lightly termed as their adventure. His eyes raised for a moment as he stared into the distance. Silver worked on a security team but that didn't keep each of the five on the team from facing difficulties and danger.

At his own place, Seamus moved slowly as he carefully cleaned the riding more, the hand mower, and the trimmers that he had used that day. He was exhausted, he once more admitted to himself. He walked towards his office, a frown on his face as he read an alert that had suddenly appeared on his phone. A missing lady. Shandy Sullivan had disappeared sometime early that day. His footsteps slowed before a hand raised to run through his dark blond curls, He thought back to that morning. Shandy had passed him as he waited to pull out onto the road, her normal morning run bringing her past his place. Shandy was a close friend from childhood. Seamus sighed. This wasn't like her, not at all. Seamus began to pray for her, fear suddenly in his heart for his friend. He decided at that moment that he would be out searching the next morning, not understanding that an upcoming event would prevent that.

Moving towards his office, Seamus sank down into his desk chair, his briefcase hitting the desk top. He rubbed at his face once more, fatigue hitting harder. End of season lawn care was always hard, he decided, reaching for his desk calendar. Seamus flipped through the pages, nodding as he decided he needed a holiday and would book that soon.

A small sound had him turning his head before he shrugged, his attention going back to his end-of-day work. Rising at last, Seamus stretched and then moved to lock his office door, heading for the outside door. Only, he didn't make it that far. Seamus turned slightly

—

before his body hit the concrete floor, the roughness scraping at his face. His vision darkened for a moment.

The two men who had tackled him shared a look before one of them reached to roughly draw Seamus' arms behind him before handcuffs clicked around his wrists. Seamus was dragged to his feet, unsteady for a moment before he was shoved forward, his feet stumbling over one another. A hand on his arm held him upright before he was hauled outside, a truck waiting for him to hit the back seat, before the doors slammed and the truck took off a high rate of speed. The men didn't say anything. They had worked together for too long and had done similar actions too many times to need to articulate that they were doing.

Seamus was pushed into a room, hitting the floor as he lost his balance. He waited, his breathing ragged, his head resting on the rough wooden floor. His eyes closed as he struggled to control his breathing and also his emotions. He had to admit that he was scared, something that was foreign to him. Twisting his body, Seamus struggled to sit upright. One knee was raised, the other ankle touching the back of that foot. He stared around, not sure what had just happened, other than that he was not at his home and his hands were cuffed behind him.

The two men stood outside the room, watching through a small window on the door. They shared a look once more before they shrugged and walked away. Their instructions had been specific, to kidnap Seamus and then lock him up in that room, leaving his wrists handcuffed behind him. Their boss had not explained why but they had not expected that.

—

Darkness dropped as it always did, the full moon and stars lighting the sky. Seamus' head twisted as he searched the room. It was dimly light by a single bulb handing from the ceiling. He sighed. This was not how his weekend was to start. He didn't have enemies, at least he didn't think he did. Shifting his body backwards, Seamus felt the wall behind him, resting his head back on it, his eyes closing as he prayed. Richard, the security team lead for his sister's security team, had taught them well, to pray in all circumstances. He sensed that he was not alone, that God was there with him.

"Okay." Seamus muttered aloud, his baritone voice startling the critters that were moving around the room. "I need to figure this out." His wrists moved as he pulled them apart, even knowing that he couldn't release them. "How do I get out of this? No one is to be around me this weekend. I won't be missed until Monday when the guys show up for work." His eyes closed, his head dropping down as he puzzled through what had happened. He had no answers.

Seamus slept, not wanting to but he couldn't control his body. He didn't hear the door unlock and one of the men approach him, a foot out to nudge at Seamus. There was no reaction. The man turned and walked out of the room, the door shut and locked behind him. He frowned for a moment. It was not usual for them to be told to leave the man handcuffed but their instructions had been specific. Seamus was not to be freed. He was to be left shackled.

The next morning, Seamus' head raised. He blinked to clear his eyes, frowning as he stared around.

—

It hadn't been a dream, after all, he thought. He really was in a ramshackle room with his hands cuffed behind him. He struggled to rise, stumbling to keep his balance before he walked around the room,

"God, where are you?" His voice echoed in the room. "Where am I? And who did this?"

Seamus turned as the door unlocked, the two men appearing. One of them reached to unlock his cuffs, allowing him a limited time of freedom before Seamus was shoved face first to the wall and his hands cuffed behind him again. His head dropped. He really couldn't escape, now could he?

Chapter 2

Monday morning brought consternation to Seamus' workers. He was always there when they arrived, but he wasn't. Not that morning. And the door to the work building was unlocked. Sam, the lead worker, stopped before he entered the building, a hand out to stop the others.

"This isn't right. Seamus isn't here." He looked around, a frown crossing his weathered face. "He's always here to meet us. And the door wouldn't be unlocked like this." His phone was out as he called for help, pointing away from the building. The workers gathered near the entrance to the driveway, milling around, worry on their faces.

Bill Butler, lead detective for the Elmton police department, stood just inside the door to the building, listening as footsteps echoed through the building. His thoughts were troubled, knowing that this was out of character for his friend. Sid, one of the crime scene techs, approached him.

"Bill? What happened here? We're not finding anything." Sid stared around, not sure what to think or say.

"I don't know. He has a security system. Silver has access to it." Bill turned as he heard footsteps approaching them and Silver stood just outside of the door. "Silver?"

"Where is Seamus?" Silver was worried about her brother. He had not responded to any of her texts and that had brought her to his home that morning. Her team mate, Stephen, had stopped by the workers, speaking quietly with them.

"We don't know, Silver. Sam says that he wasn't here when they arrived this morning, even though the door was unlocked. Can you open up his house for us?" Bill turned Silver towards the sprawling one floor house that Seamus called home.

"I can." Silver unlocked the door and then stepped back to let Bill walk through the building. When he returned, her eyes closed. Seamus was not there. "He's missing?"

"He is." Bill looked past her, studying the area outside of the home. "It's a crime scene now, Silver."

Silver nodded soberly before she walked away, finding Stephen waiting for her. He simply hugged his friend and then stood back, assessing her and then assessing the area around them.

"He's not here?" Stephen asked the question he already knew the answer to.

"No, he's not. I'm not sure when he disappeared." Silver pulled out her phone and then opened the security application for her brother's security system. She searched through it, stopping as she saw the men approaching the building. "He's was taken Friday night. I can't get much of a description of them." She forwarded the section to Bill, who turned to stare at her as he accessed his text message.

Stephen studied the clip before he reached for her phone, sending the clip to each of the other team members including himself.

"We'll find him, Silver." Stephen turned as he heard his name called. Richard, their team leader, was walking towards them. "Richard?"

'Silver? He's not here?" Richard sighed as she shook his head.

"No, not since he got home on Friday. He didn't make it from the work building." Silver drew in a quivering breath. "I didn't know."

Richard nodded, praying for his friend and her brother. He hesitated for a moment.

"He's not the only one missing. Shandy's missing as well."

Silver stared at him in shock, not sure whether to believe him or not.

"Shandy? When?"

"Friday morning. From what I understand, she disappeared on her morning run. She never showed up at her office." Richard pointed towards their vehicles. "Let's head out. Bill will find you and your parents."

Silver nodded, not willing to leave but knowing that she should. She drove off, not waiting for Stephen. He stared after her before turning to Richard, who simply shook his head.

Bill sighed to himself. There had been another abduction on Friday, he knew. Shandy Sullivan had disappeared.

That Friday morning, Shandy Sullivan had caught her auburn hair back into a pony tail, her hazel eyes thoughtful. It was early morning, just the time of day that she loved to run. She set out, waving at Seamus as she passed his driveway, catching his grin as he responded. Shandy's thoughts were troubled. She had felt followed and watched over the past few weeks. There had not been anyone that she had seen and that bothered her but not enough for her to go to Bill, a close friend.

The vehicle had stopped in front of her on the road, causing her to pause her steps and then spin, racing away from the car. She didn't get too far before arms had trapped hers to her side. She struggled to escape, just not able to. Shandy was carried back to the vehicle and shoved inside, the man trapping her wrist in a harsh grip. She just could not get away. The only thing that she could do was pray.

Shandy watched in horror as she was dragged from the car and towards a long, low, dark building. There were few windows and she could only see one door.

"No!" She protested, still struggling to escape. Her attempts to escape were futile. She was roughly shoved into a room, the narrow window high in the wall, too high for her to reach. The door slammed behind her, the lock clicking into place. Shandy ran towards it, tugging at it, unable to open it. Her hand rested again even as her forehead hit the steel of the door. She was afraid, not sure who the men had been or why she had been taken. Shandy turned slowly, studying the room with an intense gaze. It was bare, no furniture, just a curtain partitioning off the toilet and rusty sink. She sank to the floor, her back tight to the door, tears briefly clouding her vision. All she could do at the present time was pray.

Who were they? Shandy questioned herself again. Was it to do with her work as a financial analyst or something else?

Chapter 3

Seamus tugged at his handcuffs once more. It had been over thirty-six hours, he decided, since he had been kidnapped. There had been no requests for information or anything from him. He had not been forced to hold a paper showing the date. Seamus shifted as he sat on the floor, the coldness and dampness creeping into his flesh and bones. He coughed, a harsh sound in the room. His eyes closed as his head rested back on the wall. He could feel his body fading, the lack of food and shortage of fluid causing that. Seamus had only been provided with minimal food and water three times a day. His eyes closed as he slept.

The older man stood and watched him, shaking his head. He had been given no further instructions regarding the younger man in front of him, other than to continue what he had been doing. He turned and walked towards the room next to Seamus' and unlocked the door. He watched Shandy as she sat, her eyes on him. She had not cooperated with him and that meant she would not be leaving. His requests for her to sign the papers shoved at her had been met with silence and her refusal to take the pen.

Shandy's head dropped as the door was locked, fear growing within her. Her prayers seemed to be going nowhere, leaving her feeling lost and alone. She knew that the papers she was handed were illegal. Shandy would not be part of a crime and that was exactly what they were for.

News of Seamus' and Shandy's disappearance had begun to spread. Consternation and concern covered the faces of their families and friends even as the searches began. Silver and her team worked with the security team in for training, changing their training into practical and actual searching.

Shandy's home was searched, leaving more questions than answers. Bill paused for a moment, his face turning up to the warm sun even though the chill in the wind caused him to shrug deeper into his jacket. This was strange, he thought, the friends disappearing on the same day. Who had taken them, that was his question. Were they together or separate? Those were answers that no one could answer yet.

Andrew McBeth, the Elmton police chief, turned as he heard Bill's voice. He frowned at his lead detective and close friend.

"Bill? You're troubled." He pointed at Bill's office, sitting in front of the desk, watching as Bill shrugged out of his jacket and sat.

"I am. We have two people missing." Bill rubbed at his face. "Seamus disappeared Friday night. Shandy Sullivan disappeared Friday morning while she was on her run. There is no evidence as to who or why or even where they are."

Andrew stared past Bill, worried about their friend, Seamus, but also about Shandy. She worked closely with work groups at their church and he had come to know and appreciate her keen insights into life.

"No sign of what happened?" Andrew's quiet question brought Bill's attention back to him.

"We have the security video feed from Seamus. He disappeared Friday night, after he had cleaned up his equipment by the looks of it. Sid says there isn't a lot of evidence. Shandy seems to have disappeared on her morning run. We're not sure exactly where that happened." Bill was frustrated. "Jason is walking the route that she usually runs but he's not confident that he'll find anything."

Andrew nodded, his thoughts running through what might have happened.

"Silver's been around?"

"She has been. She provided the security video for us. She hadn't heard from him since Friday." Bill stood, his eyes on the floor. "I'll work it but we need more information."

"We do. I can't see Seamus having enemies but Shandy might. They've been friends since they were in public school." Andrew watched Bill walk away, his prayers raising for protection for the couple.

Shandy paced the floor, unsteady as she felt. A hand traced along the walls, keeping herself upright. She had been provided little in the way of water or even food. They were trying to break her, she decided, but had no idea why. Her thoughts turned to her personal life before she shook her head. Shandy had no idea why she would have been kidnapped. She had not been asked for anything, the man just appearing two or three times in the last few days, bringing in minimal food and water. She sighed. She finally found a corner of the room and sank to the floor, her eyes closing as she slept.

Seamus once more tugged at his wrists. The handcuffs were still in place. He had no idea who the men were, he decided, going back over what had happened just as he had numerous times over the last hours. His business was lawn care, not investments or anything that people would want. He frowned before his own eyes slid closed. He slept too, exhausted. He had not slept over the last hours and that fact had finally caught up with him.

The man stood and watched him, frustration in his bearing. His boss would be there within the hour and wanted the two ready to talk to. He walked away, knowing that he would be back to drag the two to their feet and to the office in the building that held secrets that no one knew or would guess at.

His employer strutted into the office, a hard look on his face. The excesses of his life showed in his body and face, the love of fine food, liquor, and tobacco evident. The man stood, arms stiff at his side, waiting for his instructions.

"There has been no trouble?" The older man turned, eyes narrowed as if he was having trouble seeing.

"None. We have kept the man handcuffed as per your instructions. The woman is free but still caged in the room."

"Good. Good." The employer stood for a moment. "Bring them here. I want to see them. They will work for me. Particularly that woman. We'll use him to bring her to terms."

The man nodded, turning on his heel, finding his companion waiting for him.

"He wants them here." He sighed. "And somehow I don't think it will go as he thinks it will."

Seamus felt the harsh grip on his arms, drawing him to his feet and then shoving him through the unlocked door. He stumbled as he tried to keep to his feet, fatigue and lack of nutrition affecting how much he had awakened. Unable to fully comprehend what was happening, Seamus stopped walking forward, blinking to focus on the man in front of him.

The man watched Seamus closely before he nodded. One of the men turned and stalked from the room, heading to find Shandy. She looked up as he stood over her and shrank back from him as his hand reached for her, dragging her to the feet and out of the room despite how much she struggled to resist and escape. Made to stand near Seamus, Shandy's eyes searched the room, staring at Seamus. Where had he come from? And what was wrong with him? All Shandy could do was pray for him and then for herself, knowing that God was in the room with them, providing protection for them. Of that, she was certain. Her attention then went to the man in front of her and she frowned once more. She had no idea who he was but she could feel the evil emanating from him. Shandy could barely contain the shudders that ran through her.

The man studied the two in front of him. His hands clenched the papers that he held in a tighter manner. Shandy would work for him, he decided. He needed her expertise to help hide the financial aspects of his crimes and protect those who he worked for.

"You're going to work for me, Shandy Sullivan." His harsh, rough voice broke through the silence in the room. "You have no choice. If you don't, he suffers." His head nodded at Seamus, who stood silent, listening to the words.

"Not a chance, Ivan Whyte. Not a chance." Shandy's tongue touched the cut on her lip, feeling the pain from the blow that had just lashed across her face.

"You don't have a choice, Sullivan. You will not leave here until you do." His words pelted at her, a frown on his face as he stood and hammered them at her. He didn't understand the way that she stood there so calmly, refusing to take the papers shaken at her.

"Not happening. I won't do it. And Seamus will support me in that decision. Do you really have to keep him handcuffed?" Shandy wasn't afraid to speak up. She had taken that step way too many years. Her strength of character and refusal to bend to Whyte's demands had the two other men staring at her and then at Whyte before they stared at each other.

Seamus' body jerked from the blows that suddenly rained down on him, collapsing to the floor. He heard Shandy's furious voice but could not make out her words. His eyes closed as his vision darkened. Seamus didn't understand why he was there. The demands were directed towards Shandy. They were close friends, but he had no control over what she did with her life.

Shandy stared in horror at Seamus crumpled form, her mind closing out the words lashing at her. She stumbled backwards as one of the men jerked at

<hr>

her arm, pulling her roughly from the room and away from Seamus despite her protests that she needed to help him. Shandy pounded at the door, shouting from them to unlock it and let her be with Seamus, to let her help him. Sobs rose within her as she realized that the door was not being opened and wouldn't be. Stumbling steps and the sound of dragging feet came faintly through the door. Shandy heard the sound of a door slamming nearby even as her head rested against the door. She needed to get out of there and find Seamus. Only that was not happening.

Seamus rolled to his side from where he had landed on his stomach, pain wafting through him. He had no idea who that man was but he wanted something from Shandy. He began desperate to escape, tugging at his wrists and unable to free himself. His head raised as he searched the room before he managed to sit up and then slid backwards to the wall. He rested against him, breathing hard through the hurt that hit hard at times. Seamus wanted to find Shandy and escape. That wasn't happening. And he had no idea when it would. Confusion wafted through his mind before his eyes closed and he prayed, begging God to release them and set them away from their captors.

Three days went by with the couple pulled from their rooms. The demands for Shandy to work for Whyte were escalating despite her refusals to do so. Seamus had been spared further assaults but he knew it was only a matter of time before they began again. And he wasn't sure that he would survive them.

—

That night, the moon was covered under heavy rain clouds, the rain pelting the building and the ground around it. The trees swayed with the wind, leaves flying through the air, fluttering to the ground before twirling across the grass and the gravel driveway. Dark figures moved quietly but quickly towards the building, keeping to the shadows. A hand reached out to grasp the door handle, pulling it open before the figures disappeared inside. Hand signals between then had them scattering and searching.

One of the figures stopped at the locked doors, a hand out to touch the ear piece he wore. Two figures appeared beside him before he reached to unlock the first door, a small flashlight flickering its light around the room, stopping as it shone on Shandy. One of the figures moved to scoop her into his arms, turning to head for the outdoors. He could heard the quiet conversation in his ear, knowing that Seamus had been found and someone was on the way out with him.

Richard turned from where he had come to a stop beside his SUV, searching the area. It had been almost too easy, he thought, his eyes finding Silver as she sat, an arm around her brother. He watched as Stephen, the paramedic on his team, assessed Shandy and then Seamus.

Stephen looked up, his eyes staring into the distance. He shook his head, not sure what to say.

"Richard, we need to get them assessed at the hospital. It looks as if Seamus has been handcuffed the whole time, given the scrapes on his wrists. He's been abused as well." Stephen paused, hearing the soft sound from Silver. "Both of them are weak, likely from dehydration and lack of food."

Richard nodded, slipping into the passenger seat in the front and nodding at Timothy who sat behind the wheel. His phone was out as he placed a call to Bill.

"Bill? Where are you?" Richard's voice was taut but calm.

"At the office. Why?" Bill sat back, his eyes on his computer monitor and the report that he had just finished.

"We have Seamus and Shandy. This is the address where they were." Richard's call clicked off before Bill could ask many more questions. He was confident that Bill would respond and search the building, finding what evidence that he could.

Bill stared at his phone before he was on his feet, heading for Jason.

"Jason? We need to move. Richard called." Bill shrugged into his jacket, heading for the lab.

"Richard?" Jason was on his feet, a hand reaching for his own jacket. "He has them."

"He does. He's heading for the hospital more than likely. Sid? Bring your team." Bill stood just inside the doorway to the lab, finding Sid turning towards him.

"Seamus?" Sid reached for his keys, hearing movement around him as other techs moved to leave the lab.

"Correct. We have the address where they were held." Bill turned to walk towards the parking lot, sliding behind the wheel of his car, a hand out to rub the rain from his face. Jason sat beside him, his phone out to study the text message that had just come through.

"Richard just sent a text. He said that they were locked up in separate rooms but neither roused when they were found." Jason looked up, a hard look crossing his face. Theses were friends who had been kidnapped and kept from their families for days. "Did he say much more to you?"

"No, he didn't. I don't think that he knew much. I would like to know how he found them."

"Emma." Jason uttered a name, the name of a friend who had a business where she found people and information that no one else could but how that was, she just couldn't explain.

Chapter 5

Richard paced the waiting room, his eyes on Silver and her husband, Sorley. At the moment, she was just a worried sister, not the competent team member she normally was. He knew the other three of his team members were around, Timothy with Seamus and Naomi with Shandy. He turned as he heard steps beside him. Seamus' parents were there, worry on their faces before they moved to their daughter.

Stephen paced towards him, a grim look on his face. He nodded to a corner of the room, away from the few people who were scattered through the waiting room.

"Stephen?" Richard waited patiently, knowing Stephen would speak when he was ready. Anger sparked from that man, not his usual emotion.

"Richard? What happened? And why?" Stephen's hand ran through his hair.

"We don't know as yet. Emma's working on finding more information for us. Bill's on his way here. Jason's at the site." Richard sighed, praying for his friend and his lady. He had spoken many times with Seamus. That man had had a certain tone in his voice when he spoke Shandy's name, a tone that Richard recognized. It had happened with him and Raleigh, his own wife, and the others of their friends who had met their spouses while in danger.

Saul and Meg stood at their son's bedside, her hand on his arm. The other hand covered her mouth.

Saul's arm was around his wife, anger on his face. Neither turned as footsteps approached the bed and the physician treating Seamus reaching for his stethoscope. They watched in silence as he assessed their son, worry uppermost in their minds even as they prayed for him, begging God to awaken him.

The physician stood back, his eyes on Seamus, assessing the younger man. He shook his head. He had no idea what had happened to him. Looking up, his mouth opened and closed.

Saul studied him and then studied his son. Who had done this? That was the uppermost question in his mind. Bill had been around but couldn't say much. Saul wasn't sure if it was because he didn't know or wasn't able to say.

"Mr. Sloane? Mrs. Sloane?" The physician's voice sounded loud in the room. He winced. "Seamus has been abused. There is bruising would be expected. It's the dehydration and lack of food that we need to deal with. He's on an IV now to handle that. When he will awaken? That's the unknown." He walked away.

Meg turned into Saul's hug before she moved towards the door.

"Shandy doesn't have anyone. I'm heading her way." She was gone before Saul could reply. He simply nodded, knowing how much Shandy had come to mean to Meg. To them, she was a daughter. He had seen the look in Seamus' eyes over the years, the different tone in his voice when he spoke about Shandy, and knew his son's heart. If Seamus had his way and Shandy was willing, she would become part of their family at some point.

Meg stood beside another stretcher, this time beside Shandy's. Shandy's head was moving slightly, her eyelids flickering as she tried to rouse. Bill stood on the other side, waiting for that to happen before he nodded at Meg and walked away. It would be a while, he knew, before that happened.

Naomi's arm went around Meg, hugging the lady she considered a friend. Meg and Saul had just taken Silver's team mates and friends into their family.

"You okay?" Naomi's voice was quiet.

"We will be." Meg blinked back tears. It had been bad enough when Silver and Sorley had gone through what they had. They had prayed for Seamus to be spared this.

"I know you will be. God is here, Meg, His hand protecting all of you." Naomi frowned, not sure what to say.

"We know, Naomi." Meg looked around. "You should leave."

Naomi shrugged. She knew that Nollan was in the waiting room as were the wives of her other team mates.

"I will. Richard will pull us soon." Her head turned as Richard approached. His head shook as he stood on Meg's other side, a one-armed hug delivered.

"How's Seamus?" Richard's voice was low, barely audible. He was deeply worried about his friends.

"He's still unconscious. No real injuries but he's not rousing." Meg drew in a deep shaky breath, tears once more near the surface. "What do you know, Richard?"

"Not a lot, Meg. It's early yet." Richard stayed for a while before he turned, motioning for Naomi to follow. "Head on out, Naomi. We need to be in the training facility tomorrow."

She nodded, heading for her husband, Nollan reaching to hug her, his eyes on Richard for a moment. The others quietly left as well, leaving Richard to sit beside his wife, a frown on his face. This was not making sense. Seamus worked in lawn care, not in something that would trigger any sense of crime.

"Why did this happen to Seamus?" Raleigh's voice was quiet.

"I don't know but we'll figure it out. We always do." Richard's eyes closed as he prayed, ending his prayer with his usual "I love You". "Meg is with Shandy."

"That's good. What happened to her parents? No one ever talks about them." Raleigh waited for Richard to speak, knowing that he fully thought through his words before he did so.

"We don't know. They just seemed to disappear." Richard's phone was out as he sent a text off to a friend. "I'll ask Emma to look into that, although I suspect that she has already started that search." His phone was back in his pocket, an arm reaching to wrap around Raleigh. He yawned. He hadn't slept much the last few days, spending time searching for the two and also spending a great deal of time in prayer with his Abba Father.

"You need to sleep, Richard." Raleigh watched Meg and Saul walk towards them, to find seats beside them. "Meg? Saul?"

"They're still out of it. We were asked to wait out here for a while." Saul's eyes closed, his emotions evident on his face.

Chapter 6

His eyes opening, Seamus blinked to clear his vision. A hand reached to rub at his face. He stared at it, frowning. He was free? Where were the handcuffs that had held him captive over the last few days. Seamus gazed around the room. A hospital room? When did that happen? His head dropped back to the pillow as he struggled to understand what had happened.

A small sound to his left brought his head up again as he stared that way. A softened look crossed his face, a hand reaching out for Shandy. Shandy took it as if he had offered her a life line, which in his own way he had.

"Seamus? You're awake." Shandy's voice was low and hesitant.

"I am. We're free?" His eyes slid closed again as she nodded. "When? How?"

"Last night. Richard moved in. He's not saying much." Her eyes shifted to the door. "Bill's here. He needs to talk to you." Shandy slipped away, Bill's hug stopping her in surprise. Meg was waiting for her, drawing her into a hug as well before she turned them to the waiting room. "Meg?"

"It's okay, Shandy. It's okay. No one is walking away from you." Meg's eyes were on the young man who sat, not that far from them. She knew him. A friend from another security team. Paul had simply appeared, saying that Don, a childhood friend of Richard, had sent him.

Shandy sat, not sure that she should still be there. She was told that she needed to be with someone for at least the next day but she had no one. This is when she really needed her parents, but they weren't there. They had simply disappeared when she turned eighteen. Shandy had searched as best as she could, not finding any evidence of what had happened. She had reluctantly closed the family home, sold it, and then just left that money in a bank account. The furnishings and her parents' belongings were stored in the basement of her home, a daily reminder of what she was missing.

Bill walked towards Seamus, an unreadable look on his face. His portfolio hit the bedside table even as he drew a deep breath.

"Seamus? Talk to me." Bill wasted no time. He felt strongly that there was a time limit involved but he had no proof of that.

"Talk to you? What do you want to know? That I was ambushed as I was leaving my building Friday night? That I spent days with my hands cuffed behind me? That I was forced to watch as Shandy was verbally abused and threatened? That I took abuse just to make her agree to work for Ivan Whyte? That I had little to drink or eat for all these days?" Seamus' words were bit out in anger, an emotion not common for him.

Bill nodded. This was about what they had suspected. Seamus' words had confirmed that.

—

"What else, Seamus?" Bill waited patiently, knowing that Seamus was not saying everything.

Seamus shrugged. He had a thought about what was going on but he wanted to speak with someone else first.

"Nothing concrete." Seamus' head went back on the pillow, his breathing deep. He looked over at Bill, finding his friend watching him. "Did you find him?"

"No. We just found out who it was. And I can guarantee that he's gone into hiding." Bill frowned. "You don't think so?"

Seamus shook his head as he swung his legs to sit on the side of the bed.

"He won't. He'll change his appearance enough to stay in the open. It's what he's done in the past." Seamus looked up at the door, seeing Richard and Stephen standing there. "If I can get any proof, I'll make sure that you get it."

Bill left, his portfolio tucked under his arm. He wasn't satisfied that he had all the information that he needed but he knew Seamus well enough to know that the other man would not make any accusations without proof.

Richard watched Bill walk away, even as Stephen had walked into the room. He could hear quiet conversation between the two and then footsteps walking towards him.

"Richard? I, no we, need your help." Seamus' hand rested on the wall, unsteady on his feet for a moment.

———

"And you have it. Emma and Abe are involved as is Don." Richard's voice was quiet as they walked towards the waiting room.

Meg had had to leave but Shandy had remained, her eyes closed in prayer. Paul had moved to sit beside her, alert to any danger approaching her.

Seamus' hands went out to grip Shandy's arms, startling her. Her eyes flew open in fear before she was on her feet, her own arms wrapped around her friend. Seamus held her, a look on his face that had the other men nodding, knowing that their friend had found his lady.

"Shandy?" Seamus' voice was low, only loud enough to whisper in her ear.

"Seamus? You're okay?" Shandy didn't raise her head, worried about her friend.

"I am. And you?" He felt her nod. "We're going to Mom's?"

Shandy sighed. She had tried hard to refuse, then had simply handed Meg her keys, knowing that Meg would pack some clothes for her and then just mother her as she always did.

"We are. Your mom insisted." Shandy couldn't control the tears, the tears wetting Seamus' shirt. "I miss my Mom. I just need her."

Seamus' face tightened. Her parents should be there. He made a mental note to reach out to whoever it was that he needed to, to try and track them.

"I know, sweetheart. I know." Seamus turned her and walked away, Richard, Stephen, and Paul

---

surrounding them as best as they could. This was a dangerous moment for the two, one in which they could disappear once more.

Chapter 7

Later that day, Shandy sat on the side of the bed in the guest room, her thoughts sober. Her hand raised to her face to wipe at the tears that just didn't seem to want to stop. She just felt lost, confused, worried, angry, and alone. This was when she really needed her parents and they weren't there. Shandy didn't have any idea what had happened. There had been no word. She frowned and then sighed. She had no idea what Whyte had wanted from her. Shandy had not read the papers shoved at her, hadn't wanted to know. Perhaps she should have read them but she had simply refused.

A tap came at the door before it opened carefully. Silver stood there, two bottles of water in her hand. She simply sat beside Shandy with the ease of old friends and handed her one of the bottles. Words were not necessary.

"Silver? What do we do now?" Shandy raised her eyes, to see Seamus simply standing in the hallway, his eyes watching her, a look in them and on his face that said that she was important to him.

"Where do we go? We start tracing why Whyte wants you to work for him. We start digging into his life and the lives of those around them. We look into you and your family. We look into Seamus, his contacts, his clients, those friends we never investigated with what Sorley and I went through." Silver's voice had determination.

Shandy nodded. It was what she would do when investigating someone finances.

—

"I can do the financials but someone will need to verify them." She sighed. "I want this over. I don't want Seamus hurt again."

"We can't guarantee that won't happen or that you won't be hurt. We can't control the actions of others." Silver was on her feet. "Mom has a meal ready, if you want. If not, that's okay." She walked away, stopping to hug her brother, holding on just a little bit longer.

Shandy kept her eyes on Seamus, a frown on her face, trying to puzzle out what his look meant. On her feet, she approached him, not surprised when he hugged her. She tilted her head to look up at him, surprised as he kissed her forehead. That was not something he had ever done before.

"Seamus?" Her voice held a question, one that neither one of them was ready to answer yet.

"We'll investigate, Shandy. We will work through this. Richard has already started. You know Emma. She's working it as is her team. We'll find out why." Seamus turned her to walk towards the stairs, keeping an arm around her and keeping her tight to hm.

"I know. We need to do this. I'm just afraid, Seamus, afraid of what we will find." Her steps stopped. "Why me? I mean, as a financial analyst, I look into finances and give advice."

Saul was waiting near the bottom of the stairs, having heard their footsteps coming down the oak stairs.

"Because they want you to work for them, hiding their money for one thing. And using your expertise and information to blackmail."

Shandy stared at him, her face paling.

"They would do that, wouldn't they?" Shandy shook for a moment, not feeling Seamus' arm tighten around her.

"They would. If they can find something that you have done wrong or not done, they will blackmail you." Saul pointed towards the kitchen. "Let's eat. Then we'll spend time in prayer. We need to bathe you two in that. This is far from over."

That evening, Seamus pulled the covers up higher around his neck. He had retired to his childhood bedroom, knowing that he needed to be there. His eyes closed as he prayed, begging God for protection of his lady and a swift resolution to whatever it was that they were going through. Seamus slept, not hearing the soft movements outside of the house. The men who had taken them captive once were moving around outside, trying to find a way inside.

Saul stood in the darkness, watching the motion outside. A hand reached for his phone, calling for help. Only the men were gone by the time the patrol officer arrived. Saul stood after the officer had left, not sure what was happening, only knowing that his son was now too involved in something, something that they didn't understand. His heart feared for his son and his lady.

Shandy too stood at a window, her eyes on the sky, studying the stars and the full moon. She sighed.

———

She didn't want to be there. She wanted to be in her own home but understood the reasoning why she was there. Shandy turned at last, finding her rest, but that rest was not restorative. Dreams kept awakening her. In the morning, Shandy could not articulate what the dreams were but they had scared her. Dark circles underlined her eyes.

Meg turned that morning, reaching to draw Shandy into a hug, a mother prayer whispered in Shandy's ear. Shandy hugged her tight before she moved back.

"I need to go home. I have to see what work I have waiting for me." Shandy didn't look up, expecting Meg to disagree with her.

"Of course, you do. Seamus has already headed for his own home. He had waited for you to wake up but needed to leave." Meg drew Shandy with her, heading for the door. "Come on. I'll go with you." She didn't add that Jason would be waiting for her, ready to walk through her home.

Jason watched as Meg's vehicle pulled into the driveway, Shandy's eyes on him before they flickered to Andrew McBeth, the police chief but also a good friend.

"She's going to run." Jason sighed. "They always do, don't they?"

Andrew grinned for a moment, thinking back on the adventure that he and his wife, Phoebe, had been through.

"She won't. She'll draw a line and stand there, ready to fight. She's stronger than she looks." Andrew looked around. "You've searched the outside?"

"I have. We didn't find anything but that can change." Jason reached from the keys that Shandy was handing him, nodding as she muttered the code to her security system before he walked towards the front door.

Shandy stopped in her office, staring at her computer before she pulled back the leather chair and sat, her hand reaching for the mouse to wake up the computer. She would be there for hours, she knew, catching up what she could but knowing that she would be working long hours to do just that. Her phone hit the desk top, muted as was usual.

Chapter 8

Seamus walked slowly towards his work building, not wanting to enter where he had been assaulted and taken from. Sam walked step in step with him, his eyes shifting between his employer and the building. Footsteps followed them as the other men walked behind them. It was early morning, the dawn just breaking.

Swallowing hard, Seamus reached to unlock the door and then to turn off the security system. His hand then reached for the light switch, flicking them on. He couldn't move forward for a moment, his eyes searching the corners of the room, looking for someone who shouldn't be there.

"Seamus, we've searched every day. There is no one here. Richard was around with Timothy and tightened up the security as much as he can." Sam walked away, heading for the equipment that needed to be loaded onto the trailers, the other men following him.

Late that afternoon, Sam watched Seamus as he moved towards his office. He would not be leaving until Seamus did. He found a seat in the office, his phone out to study his messages before he looked up and watched the younger man. Sam had been the first employee that Seamus had hired when his lawn care business began to take off. Sam was also a close friend, working with Seamus on church committees.

"Sam? What are your thoughts?" Seamus sat back, his eyes on the folder he had just closed.

"My thoughts? I think that you were taken to put pressure on Shandy. They want her to work for them. Money laundering comes to mind." Sam had thought this through, discussing it with the other workers. "What else? Access to financial information on her clients. That would let them steal from those accounts."

Seamus was nodding.

"I agree. But there is something more. I often wonder where her parents are. It was bizarre how they just disappeared." Seamus rubbed at his face, suddenly exhausted. "It's Friday, Sam. Head on out." He was on his feet, locking up the office and then the building. He heard Sam's quiet good night before he headed for his home, unlocking the door and stepping inside, feeling strange as he did so.

Seamus walked through his home, frowning. Something felt off. He sighed as he heard a tap at the door just as he returned from showering and changing to clean, casual clothes. He stared out of the window on the door before he opened it, reaching to hug his sister, nodding at Sorley as he moved past him, a hand resting for a moment on Seamus' shoulder.

"Silver?" Seamus finally set his sister back from him.

"You're okay?" Silver sniffed. Tears were not usual for her. Her emotions were usually under well control.

"I am. For now." He grinned briefly as Silver frowned at him before she was away, searching the house.

—

Seamus watched her, his arms crossed across his chest. Sorley stood beside him, a smile on his face.

"She's taking care of you, you know."

Seamus grinned, feeling lighter for the first time in days.

"She is. You can send her home from work but she doesn't leave it there. Not when family and friends are concerned." Seamus turned to the kitchen. "I don't know what I have to eat."

Sorley followed him, pointing at the bags on the table.

"We brought a meal, Seamus. We want to spend time with you, not cooking." Sorley reached to set out the meal that they had brought as Seamus reached for the mugs to pour their coffee.

Late that night, Seamus sat in his prayer corner, his head bowed as he fought through what he had gone through, knowing that God would be the one who walked through this trouble with him. His prayers begged for protection for his lady. That was how he now thought of Shandy.

The chiming of his phone hours later brought him back to the room. He was on his feet, phone in hand, as he headed for the door. Dawn had already broken.

Bill stood there, searching the area around him. He could feel the eyes out there, the eyes that everyone he knew who had had what they termed as adventures had felt at some point. He turned back as he heard the door open.

—

"Bill? You're here early. Come on in. I'll put on coffee." Seamus walked away, not waiting to see if Bill had followed him.

Bill shut the door quietly behind him. Andrew had sent him to talk to Seamus. There had been some developments that they needed to confirm. Bill wasn't just sure how to do that.

Seamus looked up from his mug of coffee that sat on the kitchen table in front of him. He sighed. Bill was here for a reason.

"Bill? What do you need to tell me? Or ask me?" Seamus' face tightened. "Shandy?" He was on his feet at the tap at the door, opening it to draw in Shandy and into his arms, "Shandy?"

"It's okay, Seamus. I just needed to know that you're okay." Shandy stepped back, her phone handed to Bill. 'I'm glad you're here, Bill. You need to see this."

Bill took her phone, a stern look on his face as he assessed her. She's scared, he thought, and trying hard to hide it. His glance took in the email message received in her work email. He strode away, forwarding the message to himself and also Sid. This is brutal, he thought. Who threatens someone with death without a reason? He sighed. This was something that he saw all the time. Enough is enough, he decided. How many more friends would go through these adventures? He had been through it with his wife, Cora, his first wife killed by Cora's husband.

Chapter 9

Shandy stood on her front porch the next morning, watching with amusement as Seamus walked towards her, juggling a tray of coffee and a bag of food all the while trying to tuck his keys into his jeans pocket. He looked up as she snickered, a grin on his face.

"You find this funny?" His voice held amusement, the ease of old friends in it as well.

"I do. This is just so you." She reached for the bag of food. "Let's eat on the back deck. It's warm enough still for that."

Seamus followed her through the house, setting the tray of coffees on the table and staring around. Sam had been around the day before, tidying up the yard and gardens.

"Sam did a nice job yesterday." He waited for Shandy to sit before he did and then reached for her hand to ask a blessing over their meal.

"He did. He always does. Sam's worried about us, you know." She bit into her burger, her eyes closing as she savoured the taste of the meal.

"He is. We need to talk about what happened, Shandy, at some point. Today, let's leave it behind us." Seamus bit into his own burger, his eyes on his friend.

"I think we need to discuss it today." Shandy's eyes slid closed, a fearful look crossing her face. "I'm getting horrible voice messages on my work phone that

---

are threatening me and also you. I have passed them on to Bill."

Seamus dropped his burger, his hand reaching for hers. His grasp was strong and warm on her hand, Shandy's hand clinging to his.

"You have been? So have I." Seamus' head dropped as he began to pray for them both, begging God to protect them and bring them peace in this situation. When he raised his head, he watched Shandy, knowing that she was plotting something.

"What are you up to, Shandy?" His voice was quiet.

"We need to figure this out but how do we do that?" Shandy sighed. "We're not detectives or investigators."

"No, we're not but we have friends who are. Silver told me last night that they're working on it as is Don and his team and Abe and Emma. We'll figure it out."

"I know, but how much danger are we really in? I don't know how to look back through the people I have been working with." Shandy sighed. "This is so hard."

"It is, but God is here with us. He will not walk away from us. We may not like what we have to go through but we have each other. We have many people that we can speak with."

Shandy nodded, her eyes on the end of her yard. She was on her feet, stalking that way. Seamus followed, a frown on his face, not sure what she was up to. His hand reached to stop her before he wrapped her into his arms, stopping her in her tracks.

"What is that?" Shandy's finger pointed at the box sitting in front of them. She stared at the shaking digit before she dropped her hand.

"I don't know but we'll find Bill or Jason and they'll look into it." He turned her back to the house, an arm around her, his phone in his hand to call for someone to come and take the box.

Bill stared at the contents, Sid standing beside him. They were both puzzled at what they were looking at. Sid's gloved hands reached for the photos and they were numerous. He sorted through them, looking at Bill.

"This is Shandy, through the years. It looks as if they start when she graduated from high school. And Seamus is in a lot of them, just because of how close of friends they are." Sid adjusted his stance, turning slightly to stare back at the deck where Shandy stood, her arms wrapped around herself, Seamus' arms wrapped around her, just because.

"They are, aren't they?" Bill frowned for a moment, holding what appeared to be the final photo. "This is from the church picnic. I'm not sure if they're a warning or not."

Bill walked towards the back deck, his eyes on his phone. He needed to be elsewhere but he had to have a conversation with Shandy first.

"Bill? What was in that box?" Shandy didn't wait for him to speak.

"Photos, Shandy. Photos of both you and Seamus together. Some of you on your own. There were a lot." Bill studied her closely.

"Photos?" Shandy was shocked, not sure what to say. "Can I see them?"

"We'll have you come into the department later today. Sid's working through them and will have copies ready to show you." Bill walked away, not sure what he could say that would relieve her fear and worry.

"Photos?" Shandy spun to stare at Seamus. "Who would do that?"

Seamus shrugged, not sure what to say. There wasn't much that he could say. He simply turned her back into her house and reached to make them coffee.

"Silver's on her way, Shandy, as is Naomi. They want to work with you on this." Seamus stood, his head lowered for a moment.

"They are? That's good, I think." Shandy stood for a moment, just looking lost and forlorn.

Seamus sighed before he wrapped her into his arms, his prayer whispering in her ears. She leaned against him, taking in his strength and caring. A crack was starting in her heart, a crack that was opening up to let Seamus into her heart in a new way. Seamus studied the lady who he now acknowledged that he had loved for years. She was his best friend, he knew, had been for years. He just didn't know how to protect her.

Silver and Naomi shared looks before they dropped the papers that they were holding onto the

office desk. Seamus watched them before he nodded.
They had found something, he decided.

"Before we start, let's spend some time in
prayer." Seamus found a seat beside Shandy, an arm
drawing her closer to him. The two couples with them
shared looks and a nod, seeing that the couple across
from them was truly becoming a couple. They just
feared for what that couple would face.

Chapter 10

Standing quietly just ready to react, Seamus walked the man walking towards him. He felt the evil emanation from that man. He looked around. He was on his own, having just finished the final fall cleanup on a lawn.

"You're coming with me." The voice was harsh and cruel.

"I don't think so." Seamus balanced on his feet, knowing that the man would try something. He just wasn't prepared for the blow that was dealt from behind, driving him to his knees. A look of deep pain crossed his face, as a hand reached for his back.

Yanked abruptly upright, Seamus' arms were held in a hard grip and he was pulled towards a vehicle. He heard shouts and then the men were tugging him even faster. They just didn't make it to their vehicle in time. Seamus hit the pavement, his breath driven from his body for a moment before he felt a hand on his back, holding him down.

Richard and Timothy held the two men, Stephen crouching beside Seamus. Silver was on her knees beside her brother, watching him closely, her heart praying for him. Naomi's phone was in her hand as she called for help.

Sitting up at last, Seamus looked around, a hand reaching once more for his back. The paramedics had assessed him and then left, simply stating that he needed to follow up with his own physician as soon as he could.

Jason paced the area, studying what he could of the vehicle and the men now locked into the back seats of patrol vehicles. This had been expected but they had prayed that it wouldn't happen. He turned back to find Seamus standing behind him, Richard and Timothy on either side of the man, Stephen standing behind him.

"Jason? What was all that about?" Seamus' voice held the anger that he felt and also the fear that he was trying hard to hide.

"I don't know. What can you tell me?" Jason pushed back, hearing the patrol vehicles leaving.

"I have no idea. He approached me and I just stood there. He told me I was going with them. That's when I was sucker punched from behind. You know the rest." Seamus sighed, a deep breath coming from him. "Why?"

"That we don't know right now. There is all part of the investigation. I'll be in touch." Jason walked away, needing to be on another crime scene.

Richard watched around them, feeling the watchers.

"We need to get you out of here, Seamus. There are others around." He pointed towards his truck. "In there."

Seamus paced through his work building later that afternoon, his hands working to tidy away the equipment but his mind working hard to try and determine just what was going on. He didn't understand anything at all. His thoughts turned to Shandy, his steps pausing as he walked towards the front door of the building. Seamus smiled quickly, his steps quickening. He stepped outside to see Shandy walking towards him, her steps quickening in turn as she began to run towards him and into his hug.

"Shandy? You're here?" Seamus hugged his friend, seeing his parents watching from his house.

"I am. Silver called. She was worried about me. She told me what happened earlier. You're okay?" She leaned back to look up at him.

"I am. And how was your day?" He grinned down at her, hugging her once more before he turned her towards his parents. "Let me get cleaned up. I know Mom will have something for us to eat."

Saul watched his son closely, worry uppermost in his mind. He turned as he felt a hand on his back and wrapped an arm around Silver.

"Dad? What can we do? Other than what we are doing?" Silver could only understand too well what Seamus might be facing.

"I don't know, love. What have you discovered?" He gave a sad smile. They had all prayed that Seamus would be spared the danger and threats that Silver had faced.

"Not a lot. Whyte is hiding behind shell companies and numbered companies. Emma's working through it but she's facing a real road block. She's also been called into urgent investigations."

Emma was a friend who had a business that found people and information that no one else could.

"That's not good." Saul sighed. "Who else do we go to?"

"I'm not sure, Dad." Silver moved away, Sorley reaching to hug her, his eyes searching the room until he found his brother-in-law.

Seamus sat in silence, not really listening to the conversations going on around him. Shandy sat close to him, their shoulders touching. He looked down at her for a moment, his heart on his face, before he shuttered his look and glanced around the room. His family and friends were here, including Bill and Cora, Bill's wife. He hadn't been aware that they had arrived, simply coming in as friends that night. His gaze moved around the room once more, seeing their pastor, Silas, and his wife, Madigan, there. He frowned at he saw Andrew and Phoebe as well. Seamus was on his feet, moving from the room, heading for the kitchen. He paused as he saw his mother working away there before she turned, reaching to hug her tall grown up son who just clung to his mother for a moment as he had when he was a toddler and scared.

"Seamus?" Her voice held the question that she would not ask. She didn't have to.

"I'm okay, Mom. I'll be okay. I just wish this was over." Seamus turned away, struggling with his emotions for a moment. "It's Shandy that I'm worried about."

—

"I know, son." Meg watcher her son as he wiped at his eyes, not wanting to intrude. "You love her. You always have. We have seen it in how you have protected her all these years. Don't say anything. She needs to hear it from you first."

Seamus hesitated and then nodded, silently acknowledging his mother's words. Neither of them saw Shandy as she stood just out of sight in the hallway, wonder on her face.

A week later, Shandy sat back from her office desk, watching the information on her computer monitor. Something was off about the data but she wasn't sure what. She reached back for her keyboard, her fingers flying over it before she nodded. This was not an accurate account but a bogus one someone had set up. And Shandy was afraid, afraid that this was a trap.

Turning as she heard the doorbell, Shandy sighed. This was not what she wanted at this point, to be interrupted in her investigation. A quick glance at the app that showed her security cameras had her pausing. She didn't know who that was who stood on her doorstep. Shandy crept quietly towards the door, her phone clutched tightly in her hand. She jumped slightly and suppressed a small scream as the phone vibrated. She stared at the text message, not believing what she was reading. They were friends? From Riverville?

Shandy cracked open the door just a bit, not willing to trust Seamus' text.

"Can I help you?" Her voice showed her fear, despite her best efforts not to do so.

The lady grinned, her calm demeanour helping to settled Shandy's emotions.

"Hi. You're Shandy. I'm Darci and this is my husband, Doug. We're from Riverville. Bill reached out to a friend on the force, Frankie, and he reached out to us." Darci waited for Shandy to work through her words.

Doug held up his police shield, a small smile on his face. He nodded to himself, glad to see that Shandy was being very cautious. He turned slightly as he heard footsteps behind him and reached to shake Seamus' hand.

"Doug. Darci. Glad to see you two." He grinned as he saw the slightly open door. "Shandy's not letting you in?"

Doug and Darci laughed as Shandy fully opened the door, as Seamus moved towards her, wrapping her into a hug.

"I didn't know that they were coming." Shandy walked away, her socked feet whispering across the hardwood floor. "Go ahead and make more coffee, Seamus. I need to finish something before I close down my work for the day." She heard movement behind her and sighed.

Darci had followed her, a frown on her face. She was a retired forensics psychologist who used to work for a police department until she was targeted by her supervisor, the police chief from a neighbouring town.

"Shandy?" Darci's voice was quiet. "You're worried?"

"I am." Shandy bit at her bottom lip, her arms wrapped around her abdomen. "I just found this bogus account. I'm not sure what to think."

Darci stood beside her, her eyes on Shandy.

"Can I see it?"

Shandy finally nodded, her thoughts troubled.

"I guess. I need to find someone to look into it." She raised her phone, searching for a contact name and then sending out a text message. "A friend's father is a forensics accountant. He'll look into it."

"That's good. For now, set it aside." Darci grinned. "I know that's hard. Let me tell you our story."

Shandy stared at Darci as she concluded the "adventure" that Doug and Darci had experienced.

"You went through that?" Shandy didn't hear the two men setting down trays and then reaching to move the two ladies to seats. She just moved automatically as Seamus' arm wrapped around her as he seated himself beside her.

"We did. Emma and Abe went through adventures as did all of his team, his sister, and other friends of ours." Darci shared a look with Doug. "You are not alone in this. I understand that numerous of your friends here did as well."

Seamus nodded, his thoughts tumbling over what he had discovered that day.

"We have many people that we can speak with, but for now, let's share a meal and then a time of prayer. You and Darci are here for a reason." He grinned back at Doug, who was nodding.

"Emma sent us." Doug hesitated for a moment. "Darci has done a profile for you, Seamus, Shandy. It's what she used to do, Shandy. She has an arts and craft business showcasing local artists now but she does profiles for friends. And she's always accurate with her description."

Shandy ate without really tasting what she put in her mouth. She listened to the conversation around her before she was on her feet, reaching for a pad of paper and pen. Sitting back beside Seamus, she stared at the paper before she began to write.

The other three frowned at her before Darci was sitting beside her on the couch, watching closely at the names and information that Shandy was noting.

"Shandy? What conclusion are you trying to reach?"

Shandy shrugged, not sure even in her own mind what she was trying to understand.

"I don't know. I just need to do this." She sat back at last, drained. "Here. Seamus, look it over and add to it."

Seamus took the paper, reading what she had written, and then concentrated on adding to it. He sat back as well before he handed it to Doug.

"Do you know any of these people, Doug? I have a feeling that this reaches outside of our town."

Doug was nodding as he took the pad of paper and read through it.

"You're correct in that, Shandy and Seamus. I recognize some of these names." He passed the paper to Darci, who was also nodding without reading it.

"That's what I've picked up on." Darci reached for the envelope that she had set to one side. "This is

---

the profile that I came up with." She sighed. "This is
getting old, you know. Too many of us have been
through danger."

60

The next morning, Seamus stood on his back deck. His thoughts were troubled. He shrugged deeper into his hoodie, his hands tucked into the pockets. His eyes searched the yard before his feet took him down the steps to walk the perimeter of his yards, looking for something that didn't belong there. Nothing stood out but he knew that people had been around. Shadows had shown on the security system.

Seamus returned to his home, sitting down at his office desk and pulling out his keyboard. Instead, he shoved in back under the desk and reached for his Bible. He needed God time that morning. Three hours later, he was on his feet, heading for the front door, hearing a soft tap.

Staring at Abe and Emma, he stepped backwards without a word. Emma hugged him on the way by, Abe reaching to shake his hand.

"Abe? Emma?" Seamus stared at them, a puzzled look on his face.

"We're here today, Seamus, just as friends. I am still working through what I can for you and Shandy." Emma turned from his kitchen counter where she had set a new pot of coffee. "You need our support."

"And your team? Are they here as well?" Seamus grinned at Abe as he laughed.

"Not today. They wanted to come but didn't. You know well that we'll be here if we need to be. Same as Don's team." Abe took the mug Emma handed him. "We're here today just to support you and pray with you."

"And you couldn't do that over the phone?" Seamus found a seat at his kitchen table. "I appreciate this."

"We know to a certain extent what you are going through." Abe bowed his head and began to pray, hearing soft movements as someone else joined them.

Shandy had tapped at the front door and then opened it to slip inside. She found Seamus with his head bowed as Abe prayed. She pulled back a chair to sit beside him, a hand reaching for his. She had just needed to find him that morning, the threat that she had found on her front door, shoved deeply into her cardigan pocket.

Seamus turned his head at last, studying his friend. He saw the fear lurking on her face and simply held out a hand. Shandy sighed and pulled out the crumpled paper, dropping it into his hand.

"You just found this?" Abe was nodding, knowing that would be the case.

"I did." Shandy shook for a moment. "I called Bill but he's off this weekend and away. Richard called me and knows."

Seamus read the note, fear for his friend growing even as anger poured through him. He handed it to Abe who heard it and then handed it off to Emma. Emma's eyes were on Shandy, watching her closely.

"Shandy? Is this the first one you've received?" Emma's quiet voice broke through the stillness that had followed Shandy's words.

"It is on paper. I've been receiving threats in my work emails and to my business voice mail. I just don't know what they want." Shandy blinked back tears, her emotions in a turmoil and just below the surface.

Emma nodded, her eyes on Seamus as he stared at Shandy. She sighed to herself. This was what they had all gone through, she knew, but it didn't make it any easier. She reached for the paper and reread it.

"This is vague." Abe read over her shoulder. "But it sounds familiar." Emma was lost to the group in the room as she began her search.

Shandy was on her feet, pacing. She was puzzled by what they had gone through. She paused where she couldn't be seen, studying Seamus as he sat his eyes closed as he slumped back on the couch. Shandy was afraid for her friend. She just didn't understand anything at all.

Abe stopped beside her, his head tilted to watch her before he looked around.

"Shandy? Would someone know who your clients are?" Abe's question seemed to come out of the blue.

Shandy jumped, not realizing he was there. She stared at him, her eyes wide.

"What was that you asked?" Her voice had a higher pitch than normal.

———

"I asked if anyone should know who your clients were." Abe waited patiently for her to respond.

Shandy shook her head before her brow puckered. A remembered event crossed her mind.

'You know, about three months ago, it felt as if someone was tracking what I was doing on the computer. I had Timothy take a look but he didn't see anything." She looked up at Abe. "Did I do something wrong?"

Abe shook his head.

"No, I don't know that you did. How be I have my computer expert drop over and check it out? Micah asked about that."

Shandy nodded, knowing that this had to be done. She jumped once more as she felt Seamus' arms around her and leaned back against him.

"Shandy?" Seamus shared a look with Abe.

"She thinks someone might have been tracking her computer." Abe walked away, searching for Richard who had appeared at one point.

Seamus didn't say anything, just prayed for his friend. His prayer included all the verses for peace and protection that he could think of.

Chapter 13

A week had passed since that Saturday. Nothing had been determined despite their searching. Seamus was tired, tired of living in fear, tired of worrying about Shandy. The weather wasn't helping much, being damp, cold and windy.

Silver approached her brother, reaching to hug him, before she just stood in his work building, leaning against his truck. She watched as he sorted through the equipment, packing away what he could, setting aside what needed to be serviced or repaired.

"Silver? You're troubled." Seamus looked over at her with a grin, even as he kept working.

"I am. Have you had any more threats or anything?" Silver walked towards him, shoving herself away from the truck.

"No, I haven't. Nor has Shandy." His hands paused for a moment before he walked away to lock the trimmers away in a cupboard. He turned to watch her, wiping his hands on a cloth. "Shouldn't we be?"

"You should. That says someone is watching you closely." Silver reached for the spools of trim line, setting them neatly on the shelves where they belonged. She sighed. "This is hard, you know."

Seamus nodded, knowing what she was saying and knowing to some degree what she felt. He remembered how he had felt when Silver had been threatened.

"I know, sis. Say. We need to have a barbecue." He laughed as she stared at him, mouth opening before she snapped it close.

"A barbecue? Have you seen the weather?" Silver bit back a grin.

"Yeah. We can do it." He reached for his phone, sending out a group text. They both turned as the door to the building opened and Shandy slipped inside, shaking off the rain drops before she frowned at them. "Shandy? You're here? We're planning a barbecue."

"A barbecue? In this weather?" Shandy grinned back. "When?"

"Today? Everyone is responding." Seamus reached to hug his friend, holding on a little bit longer than he should have.

"They are?" Shandy turned to Silver, finding her watching her closely. "Okay. I'll head over to your house and get started on something." She walked away, hearing Silver's footsteps behind her.

"Shandy?" Silver walked beside her, unlocking her brother's house and heading for the kitchen.

"I know, Silver. I know. I'm not sleeping, not eating as I should, and the stress is hard. I have trouble concentrating on my work." Shandy reached for the ingredients she needed for the cake that she decided was needed for dessert.

"That's what happens. They watch you stress out. If you're too stressed, then you get careless." Silver's hand paused as she worked to prepared the meat and vegetables for the grill. She could hear Seamus whistling in his bedroom.

"So, what do I do? I mean, I am spending hours in prayer and have peace that God is in control. It's just hard being human." Shandy sniffed, trying to control her tears.

"You have heard my story and the story of the rest of the team as well as those of Bill, Silas, and Andrew. I know Emma and Abe would have told you theirs and their team's and their friends' stories." Silver paused once more, a foil-wrapped package of prepared vegetables in her hand. She turned to see Seamus standing near them, listening closely.

"They have. I just don't understand how God allows us to go through things like this." Shandy paused as she shut the oven door, the cake placed inside to bake.

"We don't understand everything that we go through." Seamus reached into the fridge for the meat, not pausing in his motions. "He will use us to bring people to justice or to advance His work on earth."

"I know that He does. I still don't understand it." Shandy turned away, reaching for the dishes to wash them.

Seamus shared a look with Sorley, who had just entered through the back door. They could hear the others as they joked and laughed before the front door closed.

"Shandy? What have you received?" Sorley waited patiently for her to respond.

"Nothing. Absolutely nothing." Shandy scowled at him. "And that scares me. What are they planning that we don't know about? I hear sounds around the house at night but there is nothing on the security system. I walk down town and hear footsteps following me but I don't see anyone who stands out."

Andrew had appeared as well, listening carefully. He sighed to himself. This was typical, he decided, knowing that it would only be getting worse for the couple.

"Shandy?" Andrew's voice broke through the silence that followed her words, seeing Shandy stiffen at his voice. "We can understand to a certain extent what you are facing. We can't understand totally how you feel. We are working on it but there isn't a lot of information that we have found. Whyte has gone underground. We're actively looking for him."

"And you can't find him. And if you can't find him, then we're in more and more danger every day." Seamus sighed. "And that makes us more and more stressed. And the more stressed that we are in, the more danger that we are in."

"That's true, Seamus." Bill spoke from where he stood, his young son in his arms.

"So, how do we do this?" Shandy moved to stand beside Seamus, his hand reaching for hers. "How to we go on the offensive? Or can we even do so?"

—

Chapter 14

The next morning, Shandy slammed the back door and shoved home the dead bolt before she was running through her home, searching for somewhere to hide. She had been about to step out of the house, ready to head for a meeting, when she saw the men heading towards her, purpose in their steps.

Finding the board that she wanted in her bedroom closet, she shoved aside the clothes and ducked into the narrow opening that she had prepared in the last few weeks. She had needed to have somewhere to hide. Her hand covered her mouth, struggling to control her breathing, even as she heard the door slamming open and running footsteps. Angry voices could be heard, loud and echoing through the rooms. Shandy could not understand what they were saying but she knew that the security system that Micah and Joseph from Abe's team and Timothy and Stephen from Richard's had set up for her, including interior cameras.

Shandy sank to the floor, her head buried against her knees. She needed to creep from hr hiding place. She just wasn't ready to do that.

Seamus stood at her back door, shock on his face as he saw the shattered door. A hand reached for it before he took a step forward. He stopped before he pulled out his phone and called for help. He stood watching, his heart hurting for his friend even as he feared for her. Looking up at a sound, Seamus was on the move, reaching for Shandy.

Shandy clung to him, sobs shaking her body even as her tears soaked into his sweatshirt. He was shaken at how close she had come to disappearing, listening to the words that she spoke. The patrol officer moved away, searching as well. That officer shook his head as he turned to study Shandy, amazed that she had been able to escape from her kidnappers.

Jason walked slowly towards them, not sure what to say. That someone had wanted to take Shandy from her home that day was obvious. What wasn't obvious was who it was. They had finally found Whyte and arrested him but he was refusing to talk, even to the lawyer the court had assigned to him.

Seamus stared down at Shandy and then at Jason.

"Jason?" Seamus' voice had Shandy turning to face Jason, her face shuttered.

"Shandy? You're not okay." Jason's statement was simply that of a fact, not speculation.

"No, I'm not." Shandy drew in a shaky breath. "They brought it right into my home. If I hadn't built that hideaway,, I would have disappeared today. Do you know why?"

Jason shook his head. The evidence was sparse, Whyte was not talking, and there was no other person that they could talk to. This case was growing cold, he knew, and he didn't want that. He had spent time the day before in conference with Bill and Andrew. Andrew kept his hands off the investigations, only being involved when his advice was needed. His comments that perhaps it wasn't the financial aspect that they expected but something related to her parents.

He had asked the question that they were all asking. Where were her parents?

"Shandy. I need to talk to you about your parents. I know we've talked, but I need more information." Jason's gaze with sympathetic, knowing that he was tearing off a bandage from a wound that had never healed. It was going to hurt her in a way that she had never experienced, to talk about her parents.

Shandy nodded soberly, knowing that was the conclusion that she had reached. She had talked with both Seamus and Silver about that, Emma in on the talk.

"That's what we think. But we're not sure. I just want to know where they are. They just disappeared with no word, no letter, nothing." Shandy wiped at the tears on her cheeks, tears she hated but ones that she could not control. She felt Seamus' arms around her, holding her not just as a friend but as someone who was loved and cherished. Shandy tucked that thought away, to bring out in the darkness of a night when she couldn't sleep and wonder over.

"That's what we have decided." Jason looked around before he pointed to her picnic table. "Let's have a seat. For now, Bill wants me on this. We'll reassess it after a week. Emma is working as best she can but she's finding road blocks."

"We know. We talked with her yesterday." Seamus wrapped an arm around Shandy, just holding his friend and trying as best as he could to comfort her.

"Tell me about your parents." Jason's notepad was out, his pen hovering over a blank page.

Shandy drew in a deep breath before she was on her feet, running for her office, past the crime scene techs who were still working, and then running back to the table to sit beside Seamus. She thrust papers across the table to Jason.

"Here. This is their information, their families, their friends, their employers. Dad was an accountant. Mom taught third grade. I don't remember their families. We just didn't have a lot of contact with them. Once they disappeared, I never saw any of them. And I just don't know why." The pain and sorrow of being ignored and rejected showed briefly on her face and sounded in her voice.

Jason nodded, watching her closely before his eyes dropped to the papers and he began to read. His thoughts were troubled. He knew some of the names and not in a good way. Shandy had been spared from being sucked into a criminal family. Jason wondered that her father had been able to escape them. Had his family been involved in the couple's disappearance? Jason reached for his phone, taking pictures of the pages, and sending them on to Emma, who worked as a consultant for their force.

Shandy had been watching silently, hope on her face, hope that just maybe she might have answers to questions that had tormented her for years.

"Jason?" Seamus' voice broke the silence of the autumn morning.

"Shandy? Do you know what you have here?" Jason watched as she shook her head. "You're not aware that your father's family is into crime? That we have been watching them for years without having the evidence to arrest them?"

Shandy stared at Jason in shock, her mouth opening and closing. Her face crumpled before she was burying it against Seamus who simply tightened his hug on her, his face stern and sober.

Chapter 15

That evening, Seamus stared down at the notes he had made during their talk that afternoon. He sighed. Shandy had been quiet and withdrawn, shutting the door that Adam, a contractor friend of theirs, had replaced, closing him out. He had walked home, his hands shoved deep into his pockets.

How did what had happened to her parents and how does that draw me into it? Seamus had no answers. He could hear his phone chiming from his office but made no effort to walk that way. Instead, he stared out of the kitchen window into the dark before he drew the curtains closed, his hands reaching for his coffee cup. Seamus turned and headed for the living room, to find his favourite chair and his prayer corner. He would not sleep that night, instead holding a vigil for his friend. Seamus had finally acknowledged that he deeply loved Shandy and had for years, since they were teenagers.

Shandy turned from her front window as well, fear rushing through her. She could see the dark forms sneaking around her yard and house, seeking a way in. She stepped back to stare at the steel door that Adam had installed and rushed to check the windows and back door and then to study the security system that Richard and Stephen had updated that day.

The night crawled slowly through the hours. The men had finally left, knowing that they would not be able to take Shandy that night. Their employer would not be happy, they well knew that. Sharing looks, the two men shook their heads, found their homes, packed up what they wanted, and left town. He could find someone else to do his dirty work. A letter mailed from a town far away reached the Elmton police department three days later, containing information that was needed but also compounding the investigation.

Silas, the pastor of their church, watched from the platform that morning, assessing his congregation. His eyes landed on Shandy and Seamus, a frown briefly crossing his face. He rose and headed for the pulpit, reaching for his sermon notes before he stared down at them. This was not the message that God wanted that day. Instead, Silas moved to the side of the pulpit, leaning an arm against it. His voice rang out instead with words and verses of God's protection, comfort, and a shelter in the time of storms.

Shandy sat quietly, her eyes on the rugged cross that showed in front of the beautiful stained glass window. Her thoughts were troubled. She had no idea where she was heading. She just knew that she was still in danger and that someone was chasing her. Shandy felt Seamus' arm around her shoulders. He was doing that more and more and reaching for her hand too. She was grateful for his support. Shandy was just not sure where they were heading.

Seamus stood, drawing Shandy to her feet. He headed towards the front of the church and then through hallways until they stood outside the building, right beside his truck. He tucked her inside before he stood, a hand resting on the door, staring around. He could feel watched. Seamus couldn't see anyone though. He just felt the threat.

Slipping behind the wheel, Seamus started his truck but didn't drive off right away. He sat, thinking through what had happened and speculated on what would happen.

"Seamus?" Shandy looked over at him before looking around. "Aren't you going somewhere?"

"We will. I just don't know where to go where you'll be safe." Seamus sighed. "How do we do this?"

"I don't know. I keep asking God to remove me from this, to end it. He's silent."

"He's silent but He's still here." He reached for her hand, his voice almost breaking with his words. "He never leaves us, never forsakes us. I have to keep reminding myself that He has walked this before us and is walking right beside us right now."

"I know. I keep reminding myself too. It's hard to trust in Someone you can't see." Her voice was sober.

"There's where our faith comes in." Seamus put the truck into gear and drove off, seeing Sorley's vehicle right behind him. 'Silver and Sorley are behind us."

Shandy twisted on the seat to look out the back window.

"They are. She's looking after you." Shandy grinned briefly.

———

76

"She is. They all are." Seamus sighed. This is when he usually took a trip, to somewhere he could relax. This year, that wouldn't happen. Not while his lady love was in danger. And Seamus just didn't know how or why he was involved, other than he was friends with Shandy. Then clarity struck.

"They're after me too." His voice was broken and hoarse.

"What are you talking about?" Shandy stared at him, her eyes wide, shock and uncertainty on her face.

"Whoever is after you is after me too. Why now?" Seamus stopped in front of his garage, shifting to study her.

"Who?" Shandy was struggling to understand what Seamus was saying.

"Whoever is after you. They want me too." Seamus scrubbed at his face with his hands. "And I just wonder where your parents are. I don't think they're dead."

"I know. I know they're not." Shandy's voice was a broken whisper. "I would know in my heart that they would be. I have never had that." She wiped a tear. "I got a letter in my box this morning." She dug into a pocket and dug it out. Shandy held it out to Seamus. "It's from them."

Seamus stared at her before he was around the truck, his arms reaching her out to the ground and then running for his house, the door opening and closing behind them. His arms surrounded her, holding her tight to his heart. His own tears wet her hair, his heart

—

troubled for her, his mind racing at what and who could have done that.

Shandy shoved back from him, holding out the letter, her tear-drenched eyes on his face. He took the letter gently from her hand, not sure what would happen next. This was a step that he had not expected.

Chapter 16

Seamus unfolded the paper, his eyes not moving from Shandy's. Finally, he looked at the letter and he began to read, seeing the words of love from her parents without any explanation other than that they had been unable to contact her before. They had finally been able to free themselves but were in hiding. They were afraid to come home, afraid to approach her. Shandy was afraid for them.

"Emma." Her voice was low, barely audible.

"Of course." Seamus reached for his phone, sending off a text message to Emma with the information. She responded quickly, simply stating that she knew where they were and that Abe and his team and Don and his team were on their way to find them. Jason and Bill were also in the loop, as it is said, working through the logistics of speaking with Brendan and Rebekah.

"She's ahead of us again. How does she do that?" Seamus stared at the text message and then at Shandy, who stood, her mouth open in shock. "Jason or Bill will call us."

"They will." Shandy paced, her emotions in a uproar. "They really are alive!: She was in shock, not seeing Seamus heading for the door and opening it to find his parents, Silver and Sorley, and also Richard and Raleigh standing there, walking into his house. Saul reached to hug his son, his hands resting on his shoulders.

"Something has happened." Saul's words were a statement, not a question.

"It has." Seamus turned slightly towards the kitchen, hearing voices there, some raised in shock and surprise. "Shandy's parents? They're alive. Abe and Don and their teams are heading their way to find them. She received a letter this morning from them. We're not sure who put it into her box."

"Someone who helped them." Saul's voice was certain on that. "How is she?"

"In shock, uncertain, feeling lost. She has a lot of emotions to deal with." Seamus' voice faltered.

"And so do you. We can see your heart, son. Shandy has always been a part of our family." Saul simply prayed for his son and his lady before he walked away, passing Silver as she headed for her brother.

"Silver?" Seamus hugged his sister.

"This is where it becomes very dangerous, Seamus. You do know that." Silver couldn't hide her concern and fear for her beloved brother.

"I know. We both do. I just don't know where we go from here." Seamus reached for Shandy as she almost ran towards him, the voices still quiet in the kitchen.

"How do I do this?" Shandy didn't know what to do or where to turn.

"We'll walk you through this. We will not walk away from a lady who's part of our family." Silver began to pace before her phone was out and she was sending out a text message to her team mates. "We don't have a team in for training this week. We'll work on this." She looked up at Shandy. "Can you work anywhere?"

Shandy nodded, her mind racing on what she had pending.

"I can but I think this will be booked off as a week away from work." Her phone was out, searching for phone numbers that she needed. She walked away, already speaking to whoever it was that she needed to.

Seamus watched her before he felt a hand on his shoulder and then heard Richard's prayer for him, ending with his usual "I love You." He looked at his friend, knowing that Richard would support them and protect them in every way that he could.

"Seamus? We're working this." Richard stared out the window of the front door, watching as clouds began to cover the sky. "I remember Brendan and Rebekah. They were always so interested in the teens, not just because of you and Shandy."

"They were. Now, we have to determine just why they were taken and who was behind it." Seamus turned as Shandy's hand touched him. He reached to tuck her close to him, feeling the emotions that were shaking her body.

"Richard? What do we do?" Shandy's voice had strengthened as she struggled to cover her emotions.

"We research. We work to keep you two safe. Seamus, your work is over for now. Shandy, we set you up at our building if you want." Richard walked

—

away, looking for Silver, ready to set up the protections that would become so necessary.

Shandy watched him do just that before she too walked away, out of the house and towards her own home, not caring that it was dark and that put her into more danger that she knew but didn't want to acknowledge.

Seamus watched from the front porch, knowing that he had to let her go. He nodded as Stephen walked past him, intent on following Shandy and ensuring that she would get to her home in safety. That man paced after Shandy, eyes alert to any danger that might approach.

Richard walked to the road, studying the area around Seamus' home. Someone is out there, he knew. He watched as Naomi and Stephen walked the area, alert to any danger.

Saul draped an arm across his son's shoulders, feeling the shudder of the emotions shuddering through his body. All he could do was pray for his son. Danger was drawing closer to Seamus, just as it had with Sorley.

"Dad? Where do we go from here?" Seamus' voice was low and broken, unable to control the fear that was moving through him. "Where were her parents?"

"That's part of the investigation Bill and Jason are working through. They'll meet with them and then with Shandy." Saul studied his son. "And you will be part of it. Shandy will make sure of that."

Seamus nodded, finally walking away to find his desk chair, sinking into it. His head dropped into his hands, his elbows resting on the desk. He didn't know what to think or even where to be. He wanted to be with Shandy but had to stand back. He was only a friend at this point, even though in his heart he loved her.

Chapter 17

A week later, Shandy rose from her desk. She had immersed herself into her financial business. Something was wrong with one of her client's portfolio, but she wasn't sure just what it was. That was unusual for her. Shandy turned to study the documents still on her monitor before she sighed and closed out her programs. She walked away from her office and to the outside, a jacket drawn on as she stood on her back deck.

Seamus had been around that day, just tidying up her yard for the winter. That was what he did for her each fall. He had looked at the house and then driven away, heading for his parents' home to do the same.

Silver walked around Shandy's house an hour later, a bag of take-out food in her hands. She found Shandy still standing on the back deck, her hands shoved as deep into her pockets as she could.

"Shandy?" SIlver's voice startled Shandy who stared at her friend with wide eyes.

"Silver? Where did you come from?" Shandy turned back to her home, hearing Silver following her.

"From the restaurant?" Silver laughed softly. "You were lost in thought."

"I was. I have a client who I don't think is who they say they are." Shandy sighed. "I have to find someone to look into them."

"Try Emma." Silver reached to hug Shandy before she spread out their meal.

"I have." Shandy sighed once more, a deep from-the-toes sigh rising within in. "Has Richard heard anything?" Her gaze was hopeful as it rested on Silver.

Silver shook her head, sympathy resting on her face.

"Not yet. Until he needs to become involved, he won't. Don and Abe are working this, just because they're available to do so and to protect you and Seamus."

"And Richard, your team, and your spouses." Shandy rubbed at her eyes, feeling more tired than she had ever felt.

"That's true." Silver rubbed at the rim of her coffee mug, not sure how to continue. "Shandy? What are your feelings and thoughts on this?" She looked towards the back door as it opened quietly and Seamus walked in, poured himself a cup of coffee, and sat beside his friend. He shook his head slightly at the question on Silver's face.

"My thoughts? I don't know that I've really thought it through." She was on her feet and out of the room, returning with pads of paper and pens. "Let's try working this through."

They worked away, Shandy writing rapidly before she sat back and then was running from the room, heading for her office and the book shelves. She searched frantically, reaching for a leather-bound journal of her father's that she had never read, just placed on the shelf with a sad smile and choked back sobs.

Seamus' arm reached to hug her as she sat back down, the journal set carefully on the table in front of her.

"This is Dad's journal. I haven't looked at it ever. I didn't want to intrude in his privacy." Shandy blinked rapidly. "I don't know what it contains but we need to do this."

Seamus simply bowed his head and began to pray for Shandy and her parents. None of them knew when Brendan and Rebekah would return but return they would. There were years of healing that needed to happen but it would. They were reaching out to touch the hem of the Master's garment, reaching for healing.

Shandy's hand was shaking as she opened the journal carefully, turning the cover back. Her sobs shook her for a moment as she recognized her father's writing. She began to read, knowing that Seamus was moving closer, reading along with her.

Seamus' finger paused the turning of the pages as he frowned at a line.

"What's this? I didn't know your parents knew them." Seamus muttered the names aloud, his eyes rising as Silver made a sound. "Silver? You know them."

Silver nodded, reaching for her phone. That name? It changed everything. A quick text went to

Richard and then to Emma. Emma responded quickly, simply stating that she had come across that name and was researching it.

"Emma's already on it." Silver set her phone down carefully. "This does change it." She looked at Shandy, finding her still staring at the journal, a puzzled look on her face. "Shandy?"

Shandy shook her head, raising her face to stare first at Silver and then at Seamus.

"I don't know them. Who are they?" Her voice was quiet, controlled, but with a lost sound to it.

"No one knows exactly what they do. They stay in the shadows but the rumours are there." Seamus sat back before he reached for his pen and began making notes. He pointed to the journal. "What else does it say?"

Shandy continued to read, a frown on her face as she followed her father's thoughts. He was reading the people correctly, she decided. She just didn't know what to do with the information.

"What do we do with this?" Shandy's hand rested on the final page.

"If I have your permission, I would like to copy it and pass on the pages to my team, to Don and his team, and to Emma and Abe and his team. They will work it. It is up to you if you pass is on to Bill and Jason at this time." Silver waited patiently for Shandy to respond.

Shandy stared at her hand covering her father's handwriting before she looked up at Seamus. She found him watching her, confidence in her on his face and the understanding that he would back her decision whatever it was.

Shandy nodded, rising to her feet and heading for her office, Silver following. They heard Seamus making a new pot of coffee. That would be needed. Sorley walked in, looking for Silver before he reached to help Seamus, quiet words between the two men.

Chapter 18

That night, Seamus set aside the copies pages, tired to the core of his being. He couldn't make sense of what was going on. None of them could. And Bill and Jason weren't saying much.

He stood at last, the drapes to the front window slightly parted as he studied first the night sky and then the area to the front of his house. Someone was out there, he knew. He just didn't know if they were friend or foe.

Richard placed his phone on the end table, stretching for a moment. Don had been in touch. He was a lifelong friend of Richard's. Shandy's parents were well but it troubled both Don and Abe and their teams what the couple had been through. Don wasn't able to say, that had to come from the authorities. Richard could read it in his voice.

Raleigh's head laid against his shoulder, praying for her husband and then their friends. She didn't speak, waiting for Richard to speak. He was a deep thinker, speaking when he was ready to.

"Everything okay?" Raleigh finally voiced her concern.

"As best as it can be. Shandy will be hurt once more." Richard's voice held his emotions for a moment.

"And so will Seamus. They're a couple, whether they acknowledge it or not." Raleigh felt Richard's body moving as he nodded.

—

"They are, and they will go after Seamus to get to Shandy."

"How sure are we that it's Shandy and her parents and not Seamus?" Raleigh expressed the concerns that they were all feeling.

"We're sure of that at all. Emma has someone working on that angle." Richard tilted his head to watch her face. "What are you thinking?"

"I don't know. Who can we talk to on the streets?" Raleigh was grasping at straws.

"We'll find someone. We'll also work at protecting them but they won't let us smother them."

"No, they won't. We'll need to meet again." Raleigh was on her feet, heading for the door, finding their brothers and their wives standing there, ready to help.

Another week passed. Shandy was not sleeping, was losing weight, and despaired of their adventure as it was termed ever being over. Seamus watched her closely, taking care of her as she would let him. He finally walked away that afternoon, heading for his own home, fatigued beyond a hard's day work. He also was not sleeping properly.

The next day, Silver stood at her brother's front door, staring at the damage before she backed away, her phone in her hand.

"Bill? Where are you?" Silver's voice was shaking with her fear. This was uncommon for her.

"In my office. Why?" Bill stared at the file he was working through, a murder investigation from the day before.

"I'm at Seamus' home. His front door is broken open. I don't know if he's here or not." Silver hesitated, knowing that she could not enter the house.

Bill was on his feet, heading for his car, beckoning Jason to come with him. Red and blue flashing lights soon lit the late afternoon dimness around the house. Bill's gun was in his hand as he searched the home, seeing the signs of struggle and the faint traces of blood on the wall near the front door. Seamus had disappeared, injured to some extent.

Sid walked towards Bill, shaking his head. There was some evidence, evidence of how Seamus had struggled to escape his abductors, and evidence that he was injured.

"Sid? Talk to me." Bill stood on the front porch, watching Silver as she stood near the road, Saul and Meg beside her.

"Not a lot of evidence, Bill. There should be. It's as if someone moved in and tried to clean up hurriedly." Sid bit at his lip. "It's as if someone who knows the system is working with them."

Bill nodded. That was the consensus that Andrew and Bill had reached the night before. Jason was now working on trying to determine just who it was.

"That's what we think. Work through this. Your report goes only to me or Andrew for now. Keep your

—

computer information locked as much as you can." Bill walked away, heading for the patrol officer waiting for him before they walked towards the work building.

Silver's arm was around her mother. Sorley stood beside her father, an arm around the shoulders whom he called father. They turned as they heard a soft sound before Meg reached for Shandy.

"Silver? Meg? What's going on? Where's Seamus?" Shandy's voice showed her shock.

"We don't know." Silver drew in a deep breath. "He's not here. I don't know what happened."

Bill walked through his own home that evening, his young daughter in his arms. His son, Michael, trailed after him, chattering away, the calico cat trailing along. Cora watched them, a smile on her face but concern in her eyes. She could see the worry in Bill's eyes, knowing that one of his cases was drawing him down.

"Bill?" Cora turned to him later, the children already asleep. "Are you okay?"

Bill shook his head before wrapping her into his arms.

"Just one of my cases. I don't understand why or who." Bill reached for his phone, reading the text message and then tucking his phone away again. He would respond in the morning.

—

Chapter 19

Staring at the man standing outside of her back door, Shandy refused to open that door. She didn't know him, wouldn't open the door and put herself at risk. The man sighed. This was not how it was to go. Paul from Don's security team had been asked to find Shandy and stay with her. He knew that Luke and Micah from Abe's team were around the property as well.

Paul stepped backwards, finding Luke standing at the bottom of the stairs.

"Paul? Luke gave a brief grin. "She won't let you in?"

Paul grinned in response as he shook his head before he looked back at the door. He could see Shandy's shadow as she stood inside and watched him.

"We'll need to pull in reinforcements, I think." They both looked around as they heard another voice. Naomi was approaching them, shaking her head.

"Why are you two just standing here outside?" She stopped beside them, looking between them.

"Shandy's doing what she should. She's not opening the door to us." Paul turned back to the door, finding Shandy standing outside of it, now that she saw Naomi. "Shandy? You don't know us. You did the right thing."

"Well, yeah, what did you expect me to do?" Shandy was scared and that fear came through in anger in her voice.

"I'm Paul. I work for Don, a friend of Richard. The other two are Luke and Micah from Abe's team. Emma asked if we could be with you for today." Paul smiled in sympathy as Shandy hesitated before she turned and walked back into her house.

"It's been four days since Seamus disappeared." Naomi's voice was quiet. "We've been looking." She searched the faces of the men with her. "You've found him."

Luke gave a brief nod. Abe and Don had moved in on a property where Emma had simply stated that was where Seamus was. Shandy's parents were now at Abe's, working with authorities to find the men responsible for their disappearance and to try and come to terms with the fact that they were now free.

"We have. That's why we're here. Shandy could easily disappear or die over the next few days just in retaliation. And we need to prevent that." Luke climbed the stairs, following Shandy into the house. He found her turning and staring at him. "Shandy, we need to talk."

Shandy gave a brief nod, praying for safety for Seamus and then for herself. Her prayers then turned to pleas for protection for the men involved in all this and the women as well.

"Do you know where Seamus is?" Her voice was barely audible, full of the tears that she would not allow to fall.

—

"We do. Men are moving in to free him." Luke's hand rested lightly on her shoulder before he moved past her. "We'll get him back to you and his family."

Shandy nodded as well before she sighed and then walked away to her office. She had work waiting but she didn't want to do that. She was soon immersed in her work, vaguely hearing voices and movement through her house. God had provided protection for her. Shandy rose at last, her arms wrapping around herself.

Micah looked around as he heard her footsteps and then reached to pull back a chair for her.

"Shandy? You're troubled." Micah's words were a statement, not a question.

"I am. I feel as if someone is tracking me and I don't know how." Shandy stared over her shoulder towards her office. "It's as if someone is on my computer."

Micah's movement stopped, nodding to himself.

"Shandy? My speciality is computers. Do I have your permission to search your computer and also your phone?" Micah waited patiently for Shandy to respond, his arms crossed over his chest. He knew that Luke had entered the house, standing just inside the kitchen doorway.

Shandy stared at him. Had God just did this? Had He provided someone who would be able to help her?

"Yes. This way." Shandy almost ran towards her office, Micah following her. Luke took one look around the kitchen and then began a systematic search of the inside of her house. He stepped outside for a moment to speak with Paul, who nodded and then with a grim look, began to search outside, Naomi working with him. Someone was stalking Shandy and they wanted to find the evidence that might solve the case.

Micah studied the folders on the computer desktop before his fingers found the keyboard and began his own search. His face grew sterner as he found the hidden applications that indeed were tracking Shandy and her work. He turned to find Shandy watching him closely, standing as near as she could without interfering in his work.

"Micah? What did you find?" She was confident that he had found something.

Micah beckoned her closer, pointing to the computer.

"You were correct in your guess. Someone has been monitoring your work. We'll need to bring in Bill or Jason. For now, I would success that we set this one aside and set up a new one for you. I can grab one and put on as much security and firewalls as I can." Micah watched her closely, seeing the moment that she understood the ramifications and then her nod.

"Let's do it. Talk to Jess at the computer store. He's been trying to get me to upgrade lately." She frowned. "But it's strange how he all of sudden started that." Her face paled. "What does he know?" She shook for a moment, suddenly not sure that Jess was not a criminal.

Micah was nodding. Emma had picked up on that, he knew, and was investigating him. She hadn't found anything yet but there were some red flags that needed confirmation.

"Emma's picked up on something." Micah was on his feet. "I won't go there. I know of one not too far from here that I'll go to. It won't be tracked back to you." He walked away, pausing by Luke for a quick word. Both men turned for a moment to look towards the office.

"What about her programs?" Luke kept his voice low.

"I don't see that they were compromised but they may have been. I'll take that computer with me and continue to run my searches." Micah knew something was off about her programs, he just wasn't sure what.

Chapter 20

Saul watched Silver closely as she worked along with her mother to prepare a meal that none of them felt like. His heart was hurting, not knowing where his son was but knowing that he had been hurt. They just didn't know how bad he had been. Sorley stood beside him, praying for his father-in-law and his wife's family.

"Dad?" Sorley's voice caught at Saul's attention and he turned to the younger man. "Any word?"

Saul shook his head, unable to speak.

"Not a word. All we can do is pray and surround Seamus with those prayers." Saul sighed. "I talked to Richard. Some men from other security systems were with Shandy today. They searched her homes and found devices hidden. One of them searched her computer and then set her up on a new one."

"It was compromised." Sorley ran a hand down his face. "Was this not done before?"

"Richard said they have searched her home on a weekly basis. These were placed in the last couple of days. But no one searched her computer."

"And it should have been." Sorley reached to hug Silver close to him. "What did he find?"

"He never said. If Richard knows, he isn't saying." Saul kept his eyes on his daughter. "Silver? Richard wants us all out at the building tomorrow. He wants to go over everything that he has."

—

Silver was nodding even as her father spoke, having spoken at length with her team.

"We have been working through it. We need to get your input on what is going on." She grinned suddenly. "He's bringing in Barnabas to go over the financial aspect. He said that Barnabas was reaching out to Shandy." Barnabas was the father of a friend and a forensics accountant.

"That's good. He'll investigate it thoroughly." Saul walked away, needing to find his prayer corner. He wouldn't be sleeping that night, he knew, spending it instead at the feet of his Abba Father in petition for his son and his lady.

The next morning, Shandy walked slowly towards the office building on Richard's property, staring in amazement as the buildings and then the sprawling house. Silver walked beside her, Sorley on her other side.

"This is beautiful. I didn't realize it was so big." Shandy stopped suddenly. "I feel out of place."

"You're not. You're family." Silver walked away, leaving Shandy staring after her with her mouth open.

Sorley gave a low laugh, bringing Shandy's attention to him.

"She's right, Shandy. You're family." Sorley touched her elbow. "Now, let's get you inside and out of sight." He could feel the eyes on his back, eyes that meant harm to Shandy.

Shandy sighed. They were out there, weren't they? She was tired of this. She just wanted it all over but God had impressed on her that she needed to wait, that His timing was what mattered. She was not alone in this. God had walked it before her and was walking beside her even then.

Conversation flowed among all the people gathered there. Those of the spouses who could be there were. Papers were passed among them. Stephen finally rose, heading for the white boards, to start scribing the information that had been discovered. There was a lot but it had to be organized and then investigated.

Bill spoke quietly with Richard, taking with a word of thanks the pile of papers being handed to him.

"How's Shandy?" Bill searched the room for her, not seeing her.

"She's hurting, Bill, in a way that we both understand." Richard sighed. "Right now, she's with Meg and Silver, spending time in prayer. Her faith is what will get her through." He paused, not sure how to express what he felt. "Any word?"

"No, no word. And her parents are wanting to come home." Bill was struggling with that, unable to understand completely what had happened to them. "They have a story to tell. For now, we want to keep them apart, just for their protection."

Shandy stood that night, her eyes raised to the clear sky overhead. The stars were sparkling, reminding her of the Creator. She didn't hear the quiet footsteps that approached her before arms were wrapped around her, a hand clapped across her mouth. She wasn't given any opportunity to struggle, just carried away and to the end of the yard and through the field that backed it to a vehicle that was waiting. Shandy's wrists wee bound, leaving her struggling to escape at last. She shoved at the man holding her, finding the door handle. She jumped from the vehicle and ran, heading away from her home and to where she knew she could hide.

Her breathing heavy, Shandy found the cave that she was searching for, ducking inside and pulling the brush back in front of her. Her teeth worried at the rope, finding the knot loosening before she shook it off. She listened to the coarse angry words and the heavy steps of the running men.

"Where did she go?" The voice was hard. This was not to have happened. In the script that they had written, Shandy was to have obeyed their commands, not fight them and escape. How did they explain that they had underestimated her and her running speed? He would not accept their excuses, that much they knew. "Let's get out of here. I'm done with him." The two men ran from the area, heading for their car and disappearing, two more men not answering the angry calls that flooded their phones.

Shandy peered through the branches before she crept from the cave, searching for the men. She began to run, heading for her home and its safety. She searched through it, looking for anything that was out of order. She didn't find anything. The lock snapped closed, locking her inside her sanctuary and hopefully locking out the enemies.

———

Chapter 21

Shandy didn't sleep that night. Instead, she paced her house, moving from window to window and door to door. She was afraid, more afraid that she ever had been. Shandy jumped at each scrape of a branch against a window or the siding.

Finally settling down at her desk, Shandy paused, her hands on the keyboard before she pulled up her programs. She had to work, her clients were expecting that, despite her feelings that she couldn't. She was lost soon in the numbers that usually made her happy and fulfilled. That feeling was not longer there.

Looking up at last, she frowned at the level of the sun. It was now mid-afternoon, by the rays of the sun, and she had not stepped away from her desk for all those hours. She rose, stretched, and then headed for the kitchen, intent on finding something to eat. God has spoken to her, letting her know that Seamus was alive and would be home soon. Shandy could not explain how she knew that but she knew that God had audibly spoken to her.

Shandy jumped as she heard a small tap at her back door, turning to stare at it, fear on her face. She crept towards the door, a hand over her mouth to still her scream. She stopped moving forward in shock before she leapt for the door, yanking it open, arms out to catch the man who fell forward, a groan coming from him. Shandy hit the wooden floor hard, a small cry coming from her. Her arms tightened around

Seamus, not sure how he had ever made his way to her or where it had ever been.

Seamus' eyes were closed, his face white and pain filled. He didn't respond to the cries that sounded through the room. He didn't move, his body slack. Shandy stared down at him in shock, before she was on her feet and running for her office, finding her phone and calling for help. She was on her knees again, trying to gather Seamus close to her and unable to raise his limp body.

Blue and red lights flashed through the afternoon light even as patrol officers and paramedics ran for the house, finding Shandy bent over Seamus. Bill was there, a hand out to raise Shandy to her feet and to move her back from the activity. He watched the hurried movements of the paramedics as they worked to stabilize Seamus before moving him to a stretcher and then to the paramedic rig. It raced off as Shandy ran from Bill's grip, desperate to go with him. She stood, devastated as it disappeared, wanting to be with Seamus but not able to be.

Bill's hand was out to catch Shandy's arm, directing her to his car. Jason waved as he walked by. He would stay with the team investigating and gathering evidence from Shandy's home. He would find Bill later.

Saul and Meg almost ran into the hospital, searching for their son. Forced to wait outside of the examination rooms, they found seats beside Shandy. That lady didn't even seem to see them. The older couple stared at one another before Saul approached Bill, who stood where he could watch the three.

"Bill? What happened? All we know is that Seamus is here. Where did he come from?" Saul was genuinely puzzled.

"He appeared at Shandy's home. He's unconscious right now. They'll get you back soon to see him. For now, we need the three of you to stay together. I spoke with Richard. He's heading here with his team. Silver will be with you three." Bill walked away, his phone out as he answered a call about another investigation. There were just so many, he thought.

Silver found her parents, a hug from them not relieving her worries. Richard and the other three on their team spread out throughout the room, watchful. Richard nodded at Bill before he turned to Timothy.

"Timothy. I want you with him. Go on back."

Timothy walked away, heading for Seamus. They didn't understand where he had been or how he had escaped but that would come. For now, he was under protection and that meant Timothy would be with him wherever he went. He stood in a corner of the exam room, not watching Seamus and the activity around him but alert to what was going on elsewhere.

The medical personnel shot Timothy a look before they turned back to assessing Seamus. That man didn't move, his breathing laboured. The wound on his chest was fiery and angry, discharge slowly seeping from it. The fever he fought was high, fed by the infection. The physician stepped backwards, his eyes on Seamus before he strode from the room and to the telephone, asking for the surgeon on call be paged.

Saul, Meg, and Silver stood as the nurse came to find them. Silver reached for Shandy's hand, drawing her with them despite her protest that she didn't belong back there. The four stood just outside of the room, their eyes on Seamus, their hearts raising in prayer for their son, brother, and friend.

The surgeon turned at last, reaching for the chart and making his notes. He stood once more, studying the wound before he turned again.

"Where's his family?" His voice was low but sounded loud in the room despite the beeping and hiss of the equipment. The soft footsteps of the nurses moved around Seamus as they worked away, readying him for surgery.

"They're right outside the door." He looked that way. "You'll want to speak with them."

"I will. Who all is out there?" The surgeon looked that way as well, seeing the four people waiting.

"His parents. His sister. And the lady everyone is saying is his."

Saul moved his ladies forward, his eyes on the surgeon.

"Doc? What can you tell us?" Saul's voice was quiet but broken.

"Seamus should have had treatment when this happened. I don't where he's been or what kind of care he has received, but he is in critical condition." The surgeon went on to describe the injury, Seamus' condition, and what treatment was needed.

Saul nodded, listening carefully before he reached for the clipboard holding the consents, scrawling his signature. The four stood back as the stretcher bearing Seamus was rolled away, his face pale and pain filled as his body moved gently with the motion. Meg barely controlled her emotions, Silver with tears on her face, and Shandy with a dark stern look on her face.

Chapter 22

The day that Seamus disappeared, he had been working away in the house, doing his usual weekly cleaning. He had set the liquid cleaner away in the laundry room, the sponge set down beside it, the paper towels he had used dropped into the garbage pail. Seamus turned, stretching before glancing at his watch. He sighed. Shandy would still be working, more than likely. That meant he had to find something to do for an hour or so before he could find her.

Hearing a sound at the front door, Seamus walked that way, his steps pausing as he heard something heavy hammering at it before he spun, heading for the back door. He didn't make it. A rough hand on his arm dragged him to a halt, before he was spun to face the men standing behind him. Seamus drew in a deep breath. He knew that man, knew the violence and viciousness that he was known for.

"Mr. Sloane. You are coming with us." Whyte's half-brother, Len Whyte, stood there, an ugly look on an ugly face.

Seamus stood still, no expression on his face. He knew that if he reacted, he wouldn't leave the house alive. Suddenly, the emotions that he had kept under tight control exploded. He began to struggle with the men holding his arms, breaking free and springing towards Whyte, taking him to the ground. He felt the hands on his arms, pulling him back before he felt the slice from a knife on his chest, biting deep to the ribs before his knees buckled. Darkened floated in front of his eyes. He didn't feel himself shoved through the house and outside. He was bundled quickly into a van, the van taking off at high speed from where it had been parked at the side of the road. Seamus collapsed to the floor, his eyes closed, his breathing erratic.

Whyte turned his head slightly to watch him before he turned back to face the front. He had accomplished what he needed to do. It didn't matter that Seamus was hurt. It would be in his best interest to cooperate with them and then he would receive care. Whyte didn't understand the character of the man named Seamus.

Seamus' body was dragged into the house and then dumped into a room. He didn't move from where he landed on the floor, his eyes closed, blood dripping from the wound.

Two days passed, with Seams barely moving. His eyes would open and close and then they didn't do that at all. He lay still, redness growing around the wound, discharge beginning to drip from it.

Whyte would appear, standing over Seamus, worry beginning to show on his face. They needed Seamus on his feet to draw in Shandy and that wasn't happening.

One day, men moved in silently, hands reaching to open the doors even as the men moved through the building, searching for Seamus. Finding him, he was gathered into gentle hands and moved quickly from the room he had been locked in.

Rushed to the hospital, Seamus was moved to an exam room, the men surrounding him to protect him.

Abe and Don and their men then moved away, letting Richard's team take over his security. They disappeared, just as they always did.

Richard turned at last, his eyes on Silver. He walked towards her before he sat beside her, not saying anything. He waited for her to speak.

"How is he?" Richard finally had to ask.

Silver shrugged, her eyes towards the door to the operating suite.

"He's hurt, Richard. The wound is infected. He's in critical condition." Silver struggled with her emotions. "We have that team in tomorrow, don't we?"

"We do. You'll do what you need to do. If we have to, we'll skip your section. Abe and Don have volunteered to help. It's what we do." Richard's eyes closed as he prayed for his friends.

"I know, Richard. I just want whoever this has been." Silver's arm reached out to hug Shandy as she sat beside her. "Shandy?"

"Who is doing this? Micah called. He's tracking something on my old computer that he needs to talk to me about. It's just too much." Shandy was sober.as she spoke. "I want this over. How do we do that? Seamus has been hurt because of me."

Bill hesitated as he listened to her words, finally sitting beside Shandy.

"Why would you say that?" Bill's question broke through the silence that had followed her words.

"It's true, isn't it?" Shandy was on her feet, running from the room and down the stairs, coming to a stop as she realized that she had no transportation.

Stephen approached her, just to stand silently beside her. He waited for her to speak before he touched her arm and pointed towards his truck.

"You want to go home." His words were a statement, not a question.

"I do. I can't stay here." Shandy didn't cry. She was past that point. "I think I need to leave town."

"Don't." Stephen's voice was harsh, causing Shandy to jump. "That's what they want you to do. You run, you don't have friends around to support and protect you. You'll disappear and no one would ever know it."

Shandy stared out of the side window, mulling over Stephen's words. He was correct, she decided.

"You're right, Stephen. How do we do this? Seamus has to heal. And that will take time." Shandy grew angry. Someone was stalking her, trying to use her, "They are using me, trying to get me to do something that will cause me to lose my reputation and my license."

Stephen nodded. That was the conclusion that their team had come to. Now, they had to find out who and why. They were all working through that. Emma was as well, despite being called into urgent investigations.

"We're working on that, Shandy. We're finding information." Stephen bit at his lip. "Somehow, I think your parents are involved in this,"

Chapter 23

Shandy searched through her filing cabinets, desperate to find the information that she knew was there. She reached for a folder, hesitating before she pulled it out. Stephen stood watching her, Naomi there as well.

"What do you have there, Shandy?" Naomi took the folder, not opening it, waiting for Shandy's permission to open it.

"I think we need to look at it. If I remember, Whyte is mentioned." Shandy looked up, tears momentarily clouding her eyes. "I forgot."

"You have remembered now." Stephen's hand covered the folder, before he opened it, reading through the few pages. "He wanted you to invest in a company. That's not what you do."

"No, it's not. I don't invest in client's companies. I just look at what they have to invest and make recommendations. I trace their investments and guide them. If I am not comfortable with a company and my research into it, I don't recommend it." Shandy looked at them. "Is that why? They wanted me to recommend investments in their company to my clients? They would take the money and run."

"Or else they wanted you to approve their investments which would likely have been from money laundering." Silver paced, her mind racing with the possibilities. "Barnabas is working with you?"

"He is. He thought he might have a report by tomorrow." Shandy spun to face the two with her. "Now, we have an idea to work with. How do we do this?"

Naomi grinned at her, ready to forge ahead.

"Now, you're talking. Come on. Let's get to work." Naomi reached to hug Shandy.

"Okay, let's get going." Shandy was at her desk, waking up her computer and signing in, finding her programs and starting her own research. The room was quiet except for the tap of fingers on the keyboards or the faint rustle of paper. Shandy didn't see Stephen rise at one point and then return with coffee and sandwiches for them and then head for the door as he heard a tap.

Jason stood there, dressed casually in jeans and a sweatshirt. He was there as a friend only, his own eyes assessing Shandy, seeing the determination that Shandy had on her face.

"What has she discovered?" Jason kept his voice low.

"We think we've come up with the reason." Stephen explained quickly.

Jason nodded. That was one explanation that the investigative team had tossed around. Someone was looking into that, he knew, but they were running into roadblocks.

Richard tucked away his phone before he turned to find Saul. That man was standing and staring out of the window in the waiting room, his shoulders slumped with worry and fear even as he prayed for his son. It had been hours, it seemed, since Seamus had disappeared from their sight, taken to be operated on. No one had been out to tell them how he was and that just caused their worry to increase.

"Saul?" Richard's voice beside him caused Saul to jump. "Don and Abe are sending some of them men over to help us with security. We need them with Seamus, with you, and with Shandy. Silver will be working this. We won't be able to stop her."

"No, we won't. And it's only fair, I guess, but it's not right. Seamus shouldn't be laying there on an operating room, fighting for his life." Saul's words were harsh, the anger he felt coming through.

"It's okay to be angry, Saul. We all went through that. Just let God have it, as difficult as that it. As humans, we want to be the avenger, to bring justice to our enemies. It's hard to keep our hands off." Richard prayed for his friend.

Saul nodded slowly. That was something was what he was working through. He knew Meg felt the same. Silas had been around, staying for a while, praying with them before he left. He turned as he felt Meg's hand on his back and wrapped her into an arm. He looked past Richard, to see the surgeon walking towards them, his mask tucked under his chin, surgical cap still in place.

"Saul? Meg?" The surgeon paused, his eyes closing for a moment. He was exhausted. There had been too many surgeries over the last few days. Seamus' surgery had been long and tedious but they

114

had cleansed the wound, sutured it closed, and sent him to the ICU, antibiotics running through the IV lines to try and combat the infection.

"Doctor? Seamus?" Saul was almost afraid to ask.

"He's in the ICU now. We'll get him settled and then get you in to see him." He went on to describe what they had done. "He's still in serious condition, Saul, Meg. It will take time. I can't tell you when he will awaken."

"Thank you. God has used you." Saul didn't see the look that crossed the surgeon's face, shock that he would be told that.

Meg hugged her husband before she searched for Silver, drawing her daughter into a tight hug. Both wiped at their faces, tears of relief and fear tracking down their cheeks.

Richard walked away, his phone out to call Stephen.

"Stephen? Where do we stand?" Richard found a quiet corner where he could watch Seamus' family.

"We're looking into that angle of money laundering." Stephen paced away from the office. "Shandy had a file on the Whyte's that she had forgotten about. We're trying to track them but there are a lot of roadblocks."

"That's what we found." Richard's mind was racing, finding Silver standing beside him. "What if their name isn't Whyte?" Silver was nodding at his words, that being the conclusion that she had come to.

"Okay. Emma's working that I know." Richard tucked away his phone, his thoughts troubled. "Silver?"

"I want in on the investigation but I want to be here too." Silver was torn.

Chapter 24

Seamus's head twisted on the pillow two days later, a hand reaching for his chest to cradle it against the pain that he felt. His eyes opened and he stared around, blinking to try and clear his vision. That didn't work as he drifted off into a real sleep.

Meg watched her son, a hand on his, prayers raising. They had not expected him to be awake yet. The nurses moved around the bed before they walked out, turning briefly to study Meg and her son.

Shandy moved silently through the hospital corridors that evening, heading for Seamus. She hesitated before she walked through the door, her head twisting as she felt watched but not seeing anyone. She shivered with the fear that flowed through her.

Stopping by the bed Shandy studied her friend, releasing that he was beginning to break down the wall she had around her heart. Her dreams from her teens, that he was always with her, began to rise again. Her hand reached to rest on his, stopping the restlessness of it.

Seamus moaned as he awakened, his hand turning to grip the hand covering his. It was Shandy's, of that he was certain. He studied the room, a hospital room he decided, not sure why he was there. His chest hurt and his free hand found the wound, poking at the bandage before another hand moved his away from it.

"Seamus?" Shandy's voice was low, almost as if she was afraid that she was seeing things.

"Shandy?" Seamus had to lick at his lips and clear his throat before the words came out. "Where am I? What happened?"

"You're awake. We didn't expect you to be wake yet. You're in the hospital. You disappeared a few days ago and were stabbed at that time. We didn't know where to find you." Shandy blinked rapidly.

"I am? I was? I don't remember." He squinted up at her. "Are you okay?"

"I am. We were so worried." Shandy turned and ran from the room, not listening as Seamus called for her to stop and come back.

Seamus struggled to rise, the pain and weakness preventing that. His head flopped back on the pillow as his eyes closed. All he could do was breathe hard and try to work through the pain. His thoughts turned to prayer, the only thing that he was capable of at that moment.

Shandy ran from the hospital, finding her car and then just driving aimlessly, not sure where she wanted to be or what she wanted to do. She finally ended up at a coffee shop, a cup of coffee on the table in front of her, her back slumping against the booth seat back. She was scared, she had to admit, the information that they were discovering more and more frightening. Shandy knew that she had been targeted. She just didn't know who or why. They had come to the conclusion that the Whyte's were part of it. They just hadn't figured out who was behind him. And they had no idea who had taken Seamus from his home. Seamus had not been able to provide much information, despite Jason's repeated talks with him.

The next morning, Shandy paced her back yard, studying the flower beds that had been cleared or cut back for the winter. Whatever she was facing was taking too much of her thoughts and times. She sighed. Shandy walked back into her house and then through it, reaching for her purse and tucking her phone inside. She was due at a Bible study for working ladies and really didn't want to be there. Force of habit had her driving towards the church, not seeing the truck that tailed her before it pulled in after her and the man dropped down to follow her inside. Don had volunteered that morning to follow Shandy, knowing that she was troubled and not likely aware of who was around her. This was when she could disappear.

Shandy walked away from her friends that morning, a troubled thought driving through her mind. Something that had been said in their Bible study on protection had caught her attention. She wanted to be in her home where she felt safe and start a study on God's protection.

She finally set aside her Bible, her thoughts peaceful for a moment. God had been speaking to her, reminding her of His presence. Hungry for once, she was on her feet, heading for the crockpot that she had plugged in that morning, sniffing at the delicious aroma of chili that filled the kitchen. Turning as she heard a tap at the door, Shandy frowned. She was not expecting anyone.

Looking through the window on the door, Shandy frowned. Abe and Emma stood there.

Opening the doors, she paused before they entered, both hugging her.

"I was just about to eat." Shandy headed for the kitchen. "You can join me if you like."

"It's okay, Shandy. Just coffee and tea is fine for us." Emma reached to make her tea, seeing Abe pouring coffee for himself and Shandy.

Abe's voice filled the room as he prayed for his friends. Afterwards, Shandy maintained that she was brought right to the throne of God. She looked up at them when Abe finished before she began to eat.

"Shandy? You've been okay?" Abe asked the question that needed to be asked.

"I am. Thank you. I spent time with God today. He's in control and will protect. I may not like what I face but I will face it with Him and with my friends." She paused, her eyes on him. "I know what you went through. You've told me. I have no idea what Seamus and I are facing but we are not alone."

"No, Shandy, you are never alone. We are all walking this with you. We don't know exactly what you are facing. No one here is able to do that. Each adventure is unique to each couple." Emma reached to grasp Shandy's hand. "Now, what have you discovered? Other than that you are protected by God."

Shandy smiled, a genuine smile this time that reached to her eyes. She finally felt a peace in the situation despite the ongoing danger. She reached for the papers that Emma had laid on the table.

"What did you find, Emma?" Shandy read through the paperwork, a frown on her face. "Mom and Dad are involved? Are they innocent?"

Abe and Emma shared a look. This was what they were trying hard to determine and those facts were still hidden under layers of paperwork.

"We don't know, Shandy. We are trying to determine that but are running into many road blocks." Abe sighed. "That's why we have them somewhere safe and won't connect you two until we have confirmed everything. They are somewhere safe."

"I see." Shandy sat quietly, her thoughts muddled. "Where do we go from here?"

"We continue to investigate. Our friends are weighing in. Kat, Micah's wife, has a family tree program that she is working through. Another friend, Darci, is working on a profile for us. She and her husband, Doug, are planning on coming through in the next few days to go over it with you. She'll provide it to Bill as well."

Shandy closed the door between Abe and Emma later, her hand twisting the lock on the door. She should be heading for the hospital, but she just didn't have the heart to do that. She instead headed for her bedroom and then to sleep. Her emotions were to the point that she felt she couldn't cope any more.

Chapter 25

Seamus walked carefully into his home, fear flickering through him as he entered the space where he had been assaulted and then disappeared from. He walked through his house, his father watching him, noting how slow Seamus was walking.

Meg turned from the kitchen counter, worry for her son uppermost in her mind. She knew that Silver would be around when she finished her work. She just didn't feel safe. They had no idea who was behind the assault and that meant they were unable to take all the precautions that they could.

Saul turned back to Meg, wrapping her into a hug. They had spent many hours in prayer, begging God to end this adventure. It just wasn't happening. They had to trust God enough to know that He only wanted the best for Seamus and Shandy.

Seamus sat on his bed, staring at his bare feet. He needed to pull on socks but felt just too weak to do that. He looked around, seeing Bill standing there, just wanting him before he reached for the black wool socks and pulled them onto Seamus' feet. He stood back before his hand helped Seamus to his feet.

"Seamus? Should you be home?" Bill's hand kept Seamus on his feet.

"No. They wanted me to stay longer. I just couldn't." Seamus swayed on his feet, his hand on his chest. The pain was coming in waves and he felt nauseous from it. "I want this over, Bill. They almost killed me." He hesitated before he continued. "Who did this? And how does it connect with Shandy?"

Bill nodded. Seamus had gone to the centre of the investigation.

"We're working that way, Seamus. It's not over, and won't be for a while." Bill walked away at last, heading for his office and all the investigations that were waiting for him.

Andrew watched Bill for a moment before he entered that man's office and sat, just waiting for Bill to look up.

"Andrew? Where would you go?" Bill sat back, rolling his pen in his fingers.

"Where would I go? You've investigated all his workers, his contacts, his suppliers?" Bill nodded at that. "Then I would continue to dig deeper, expanding my investigation to the people involved with those you have investigated. It's a big investigation, Bill. Pull in who you can." Andrew hesitated before he continued. "I have no idea where you're heading but I can guess. Where do her parents appear in all this?"

"That's a good question, Andrew." Bill drew a deep breath. "There are inconsistencies in their stories, not quite matching what Shandy has told us about her early life. Abe had agreed to keep them at his compound. Frankie Brennan is working through that part of the investigation." Frankie was the lead detective on the Riverville force and a good friend to Bill.

"He'll work it through, not leaving a stone unturned." Andrew rose and walked away, intent on finishing the paperwork on his desk and hopefully heading home on time that day.

Late that night, Seamus sank down in his desk chair. He needed to rest but his thoughts were driving him to investigate what he could. He pulled up his email and began to read through the messages that was waiting for him. His hand froze on the mouse as he read the one that was sent the day that he disappeared. He frowned before he forwarded it on to Emma and Bill. This was a direct threat against him and also Shandy. Seamus sat back, his thoughts whirling. Who had sent this? He looked at the email address the message came from. It made no sense at all.

His hand reaching for his phone, Seamus simply called Shandy, waiting impatiently until he heard her voice.

"Shandy? Are you okay?" He waited impatiently for her to respond.

"I am. Just really scared. I can hear movement outside of the house but nothing is showing on the security system. The patrol officer walked around but there wasn't anything there. He said someone would be around in the morning." Shandy's voice was quiet, subdued.

"I wish I could take that from you." Seamus stated. "How do we do this?" His voice was low and broken. "Shandy, we need to talk."

"Talk? About what?" Shandy curled up on her couch, pulling a blanket over herself, her hand gripping the edge of it tightly.

"About us." Seamus sighed. "This is a conversation we need to and should be having in person. I love you, Shandy. I want to spend the rest of my life with you." His voice faltered, not sure that he should have even spoken.

Shandy stared at her phone in shock. Had he really said that? Her mouth opened and closed before she could speak.

"Seamus? Did you really say that?" Shandy could imagine his nodding before she spoke. "I love you too."

Seamus' eyes closed. His body was shutting down and he knew that he needed to end the call.

"I do love you. We'll talk tomorrow. Have a good sleep, sweetheart." Seamus clicked of the call and set his phone on the night stand, his eyes closing as he lay down and pulled the covers up to his ears. He was asleep, a smile on his face.

Shandy sat quietly, just a low light on in the living room. Her face was dreamy, forgotten and buried dreams coming once more to the surface. They would talk, she knew, but for tonight, their declared love was enough. All Shandy could do was thank her Abba Father for bringing something into her life that was just for her.

The next morning, Shandy stood in her back yard, watching as a patrol officer walked her yard and then around her house before he approached her.

"Shandy? Someone has been around. It looks as if they were trying to get in." Tim was a friend from school.

"I know. That's what I thought." Shandy shifted on her feet. "What do I do, Tim? We've upped the security as much as we can. I can't leave my home." Her words were sober.

"No, you can't. And I know that you would have done everything to keep you safe." Tim paused, his hands gripping at his vest. "Who hates you that much, Shandy? What about your parents? Who hates them enough to make them disappear and drive you to this?" He walked away at last, troubled at the threat racing towards his friend.

Seamus walked towards her late that afternoon, reaching to hug her tightly as she turned to him. Her face raised to him and he simply kissed her, and then held her, feeling the shudders working through her body.

Shandy finally shoved back from him, her eyes looking everywhere but at him. His arms held her gently, a prayer whispering just for her. They would talk, he muttered but first, would she go out for a meal with him?

Chapter 26

A week later, Seamus stood in his work building before walking to that office in there. He sank into his chair and then pulled his keyboard towards him, bringing up his schedule He sighed. This was not what he wanted to do.

Seamus rose, walking through his building, checking on equipment that he would not be using until the spring. He turned instead to the winter equipment, hands resting on a snowblower, not sure if it would be used at all that year.

He turned as he heard footsteps, fear causing him to hesitate where he was hidden. He sighed. Bill had appeared, dressed casually.

"Bill?" Seamus stepped around the equipment, a questioning look on his face.

"Seamus? I wondered where you were." Bill grinned at he looked around the service area of the building. "You're ready for winter?"

"I am. The guys are ready as well." Seamus rubbed at his chest. The wound was healing but it would take time to completely. His strength would also take time to return.

"That's good. I'm not here as your investigator, Seamus. I'm here as your friend. Can we talk?" Bill waited outside as Seamus locked up his building and then walked quietly towards the house.

Taking the mug of coffee handed to him, Bill walked through Seamus' house, searching for anything that was out of order. He didn't see anything. Seamus watched him. This was Bill being Bill, taking care of his friends.

"Seamus? What can we do for you?" Bill returned to the kitchen, setting his mug on the counter, his arms crossing across his chest as he leaned against it.

"What can you do for me? I'm not sure that I understand." Seamus was genuinely puzzled by that question, forgetting how their friends took care of one another.

"Yes. What do you need? Other than for this to be over." Bill sighed. He reached into his pocket, pulling out a folded paper. "Frankie was through today. He left this for you." He held out his hand.

Seamus stared at the paper, not sure if he should take it or not.

"What's this?" Seamus' eyed his friend, knowing that Bill would not answer. He sighed and took it, unfolding it. He read it, a frown on his face. "What's this?"

"A promise and an offer." Bill nodded at it. "That's from the Barnabas Foundation, a foundation that offers encouragement. That is Barnabas Carey's number. He wants to speak with you. Each one of the men he employs, including himself, had adventures just like you are going through. He wants to meet with you as well, with you and Shandy. All you have to do is listen."

Seamus read the note once more, just a simple request for Seamus to call him and the request that Shandy be with him when he did. He tucked the note away, needing to pray over the request.

Their discussion turned to the messages that Silas was bringing, those of God's protection and aid in times of trouble.

Seamus headed for Shandy late that afternoon, his eyes on his watch. She should be done her work, he decided, tapping at her door and waiting for her to answer. Shandy opened the door, her phone to her ear, and pointing towards her office. He nodded, heading for the kitchen instead. An aromatic smell filled the kitchen, rising from the crockpot on the counter. She had set something for a meal for them to share.

Shandy watched Seamus closely, sensing something had changed. She finally reached out a hand, resting it on his and stopping the restless movement of his.

"Seamus? What happened?" Her voice was low as she asked that question, knowing somehow that when he spoke things would change.

Seamus pulled out the paper, handing it to her without any words. She read it, a frown on her face, before she looked up at him.

"What is this?" Shandy read the letter again.

"I don't know. Barnabas Carey runs the Barnabas Foundation, a Foundation that provides encouragement to others. We need to call him." Seamus reached for his phone, setting it on the table before he reached to wrap her in his arms. His prayer reached heavenwards, asking for peace and understanding in his words.

Seamus' fingers trembled slightly as he found the numbers on the keypad and then hit the connect button. He put the phone on speaker, an arm around Shandy.

"Barnabas Carey." The voice was firm but warm.

"Mr. Carey? This is Seamus Sloane." Seamus could hear the rustling of paper as he waited.

"Seamus. Thank you for calling. I gather that Shandy is with you." Barnabas had no doubt that she was. "I did need to speak with you. I understand that you are going through something right now. We can understand to some degree. However I do need to speak to you about a business proposal from our board. Can we meet at some point this weekend?"

"I guess. Tomorrow?" Seamus stammered at he spoke.

"That works. My wife, Aubrey, and myself can head your way. May I have your address?" Barnabas took the notes he needed before he concluded his call.

"Seamus?" Shandy's voice had questions and wonder. "Did he say a business proposal?"

"He did. I don't know what that would be." Seamus stared at her before he wrapped her into a hug. 'You know, I've been wanting to do something else but I have no idea what. And so have you."

"I have been. I'm not happy doing what I am now. Part of it is what we're going through." Shandy rested against Seamus, struggling to understand what they were to be told.

"I know. We need to pray this over." Seamus rose at last, their meal over, a time spent in prayer. "Lock up after me, sweetheart. I'll be here in the morning."

Shandy clicked the lock on the door, locking herself in. She stared at it, wondering if the lock on her life would ever disengage. She looked up, begging God to release her and let her live the life that she was meant to live. A peace settled over her as she felt the hand of God on her.

Seamus turned from his front window in the middle of the night. There were no lights on in the house, leaving the only light from the moon. He was puzzled t the request to meet with Barnabas. He didn't know why he had been approached and looked forward to meeting with Barnabas with eager anticipation and also concern.

Barnabas turned from his desk. He too had been awake, reading back through the proposal that the board had prayed over and then prayed over someone to run it. They didn't know Seamus but they knew of him. Dallas, a retired detective and close friend, had researched him at Barnabas' request, finding nothing that but a good character.

Chapter 27

That Saturday afternoon, Shandy paced Seamus' house. She had been receiving vicious emails to her work account over the night and into the afternoon. She had passed them on to who they needed to go to but she was terrified. Seamus had hugged her and then walked away to stand on the front porch, watching the area around him for anyone wanting to harm his lady.

Shandy began to pace the house, her left hand held in front of her. A beautiful ruby ring now rested on her ring finger. She sighed. Life was going on but the danger was growing. She sensed that more than knowing for sure.

Seamus watched her, a sigh rising from him as well. How did they do this? How did he keep her safe and yet let her have the freedom that she needed? He turned as he heard a tap at the door, heading that way, pausing to look through the window.

Opening the door, Seamus reached to shake Barnabas' hand and then Aubrey's. He stepped back to let them in, shutting the door behind them. He knew that somehow their visit would change his life. He just didn't know how.

An hour later, seated at the kitchen table, Barnabas looked up from their time of prayer. He reached for a folder that he had set to one side before he studied the couple across from him.

"Seamus. Shandy. You are wondering why we are here. We understand that you are going through an adventure similar to what we and others have shared. This?" He touched the folder. "Our board has been aware of a need in your town. Someone from here approached us with a concern. Seamus, we know that you are in the lawn care business. There is a need for aid in that area. There are many seniors, single parents, low-income people, and disabled people who struggle to maintain their homes. The board has agreed among themselves. They want to set up a charity here that would address that need. The board has spent time in prayer and your name has come up for that position. Shandy? I don't know how content you are with your work. Your name has come up as a companion to Seamus in this, working with the same demographic group in financing. We don't expect an answer today. Take the time to pray over it. There is no time line to your answer. You let us know. If either of you refuse, then we pray for someone else."

Barnabas and Aubrey stayed for a while longer before they walked away, the folder left on the kitchen table. Shandy's finger touched it lightly. It seemed to be an answer to her prayer for change but she wasn't sure if that was what she wanted to do.

Seamus sat beside his lady, an arm around her and his head resting against hers.

"I didn't expect this." His voice was quiet, a tone of shock still in it.

"I didn't either. I have heard this is what they do." Shandy shifted slightly, to study him. 'What are your thoughts?"

"This is what I have wanted to do but just didn't have the resources to do so. There are so many possibilities in this." Seamus' thoughts were racing as he reached once more for the folder.

"It will take a lot of prayer, that I know. This is what I have wanted to do as well." Shandy leaned harder against him. "How do we do this with what we are going through?"

"God knows, sweetheart. God knows. He's working it all out for us." Seamus was on his feet, reaching for her hand. "Come on, sweetheart, I'm taking you out to dinner."

The next day, Shandy set aside her work, She just had no interest in that work anymore. Instead, she reached for a pen and a pad of paper, heading for the living room. She was soon lost in plans for a new line of work, one that had interested her for years, that of helping the disadvantaged.

Shandy didn't hear the disturbance outside, the calls of the police officers that moved in and arrested the men who were creeping towards her home, intent on taking her captive once more. She jumped as she heard the tap at her door, a hand to her mouth to cover her scream.

Creeping slowly towards the door, Shandy's head dropped as she saw Jason standing here, a grim look on his face.

"Jason?" She stepped backwards as he moved forward, shutting the door behind him.

"Shandy? Did you know there were men outside intent on abducting you again?" Jason watched her intently.

"There were? And no I didn't. I was working on something." Shandy stalked away from him only to spin and stalk back. "And you've arrested them."

"We have. A patrol officer spotted them moving in and called for assistance. If he hadn't seen them, you would have disappeared again. What are we to do?" Jason was at a loss, as were the other investigators. They just couldn't catch a break where Seamus and Shandy were concerned.

Shandy sighed. How were they to solve this without further danger coming to them? She knew that she was being followed when she was out and about, even when she was with Seamus. She worried about him, worried about his family and friends, that they would be hurt because of her.

"Jason? Can I ask you something? How do we know exactly who this is directed at?" She watched Jason as he looked down, a look crossing his face that she couldn't understand.

"We don't know for sure, Shandy. We think it's you or Seamus. We're just not sure. We have not found any information that directly confirms that."

"Then, you need to start looking further, into others. We may be a smokescreen, just to confuse the issue." Shandy closed and locked the door behind him, a frown crossing her face. She would need to talk to Seamus about that but he was out of town for the day, away at a conference that he had signed up for months ago. He would not be back for three days. Shandy worried about him, not sure if he was even safe.

Silver stood for a moment, staring at the plate she held in her hand. Sorley wrapped an arm around her, just waiting for her to speak.

"Sorley? How safe are they? And just why were they targeted?" Silver was highly worried about her beloved brother and his lady. Things were still at the moment in their adventure. She understood only too well that it would get more dangerous for them.

Chapter 28

Seamus parked in front of his garage three days later. He was exhausted, the conference being intense but well worth the time. His head rested against the headrest of the seat, his eyelids sliding closed. He needed to enter his home. He was just reluctant to.

Slipping down to the ground, Seamus reached for his duffel bag, heading for the back door. Unlocking it, he stepped inside, keying off the security system and heading for the laundry room to drop the bag to the floor. He reached for his phone, scrolling through his voice mail and text messages, frowning as he didn't see any from Shandy. He spun, running for his truck, the house door locked behind him before he was speeding towards his lady, fatigue forgotten.

Hammering at her front door, Seamus drew in a deep breath. Her car was there. Where was she? He ran for the backyard, sliding to a halt as he saw her simply sitting in her arbour, her head resting against her upraised knees. He slipped to a seating position beside her, prayers raising that she was safe.

"Seamus? You're home?" Shandy reached to hug him, content to be held.

"Yeah. Just got home." Seamus waited for his heart beat to return to normal. "I thought something had happened to you."

Shandy shook her head. She knew that she had not reached out to him, not realizing how worried that would make him.

"I took a break from all my digital stuff. I'm sorry." She sniffed, not wanting to cry in front of him.

"How bad were the messages?" Seamus went right to the centre of the problem.

"Bad. I'm sent them on but they just wouldn't stop." Shandy was almost at the limit of what she could humanly take. "I want this over, Seamus. We need it over." Sobs began to shake her body, driving him to wrap her tightly to his body.

"I know, sweetheart. I know." Seamus bit at his lip, a habit that he had developed over the last few weeks, a sign of uncertainty. He waited until her sobs ceased, despite the hiccups that randomly shook her body. "Sweetheart, I want to ask you something. We've been praying over our relationship and when we marry. Will you marry me now?"

Shandy's motions stilled, her hand gripping his. This is what she had expected to come, just not so soon. She shoved back enough to look up at him.

"Do you mean that?" Seamus refused to look at her. A hand reached to touch his face. "I will, Seamus. I want what time we have. We don't know how long we have."

Seamus finally looked at her before he kissed her. He was afraid for her, afraid for himself, and afraid for their family and friends.

"What about your parents?" Seamus had to ask.

"They're not here. I don't want to wait for months until they have explained themselves. I have gotten used to them not being there." Shandy reached for his phone, pulling up his calendar application. "Let's pick a date."

Seamus stood in his parents' home that night, almost floating. Saul and Meg studied him and then studied one another.

"Seamus?" Meg finally broke into his thoughts. "What is going on?"

"Shandy and I have set a date. We have decided that we don't want to wait." Seamus hugged his mother. "Mom?"

"She needs a mother to help. I'll find her tomorrow." Meg walked away, troubled in her mind about the step her son had chosen but knowing that he would have prayed it through. She reached for her phone, her finger hesitating for a moment before she made that call. "Shandy? It's Meg. Seamus said you have set a date."

Shandy struggled with her emotions, desperately wanting her mother but knowing she wasn't there. Meg was offering to step in.

"We have. I have to find a dress." Shandy rubbed at her countertop with a slim forefinger.

"And you want a mom with you. Will tomorrow work?" Meg prayed for her daughter to be, bringing a sense of peace to Shandy.

The next morning, Shandy stood on the sidewalk, Silver's arm around her, as she stared at the bridal shop. She was reluctant to move forward. Meg drew Shandy forward, watching as the younger lady found a dress.

Richard turned as Seamus walked towards him. He stood outside of his training building, Stephen and Timothy standing nearby. Naomi had left to find the other ladies.

"Seamus?" Richard's voice brought Seamus' head up. He grinned at him. "Silver said you set a date."

"We did." Seamus shoved his hands into his jacket pocket. "I'm not sure if we should but we have both prayed about it." He sighed. "We want this over but we don't know where we stand that way."

"It's to be expected." Richard pointed towards his office building. "We've been working on it. Let's head in and you can see what we've found."

Seamus walked through the room, reading what was written on the white boards. He nodded. The team were heading towards what they had determined.

"You're sure about this?" Seamus' finger tapped at the last board and the names written there.

"We are." Timothy perched on the corner of a table, crossing his arms over his chest. "Are you?"

"We are. This is what Shandy and I have determined. Jason and Bill seem to be heading that way as well." Seamus turned to face the other three men. "We need to end this. How do we do that?"

"We continue to work this as we have been." Richard tapped the board as well. "These people? They're hiding in plain sight. We will find the information that is needed. Emma is working on that as well. She's finding names and other information that she wants to talk with you about."

Seamus nodded. This is where God would step in, he acknowledge. He would lead them to the information and the confirmation that they needed. He would protect them and guide them.

"Okay. We continue this. You have teams in for training. I'm at loose ends right now. Can I work from here?" Seamus asked, knowing already what the answer would be.

"Of course you can. We'll work with you as we can." Stephen didn't need to look at Richard to know he was nodding. "What about Shandy?"

"She's taking a break from her work. She's not sure if she wants to continue with that." Seamus rubbed at his face. "We've praying through another offer of work that would mean we work together. I would covet your prayers for that."

The other three nodded, Richard simply bowing his head to pray for Seamus and Shandy. Seamus walked away at last, feeling comforted and protected for once.

Chapter 29

Two weeks later, Shandy moved through Seamus' home. They had married the day before but had chosen not to leave town for a honeymoon. They didn't feel safe doing that, thinking that they would be putting others in danger if the men followed them. And follow them they would. Shandy turned as she heard Seamus' whistle in the kitchen. He was working on a meal for them, the aroma of tomato sauce spreading through the house and making Shandy hungry.

She walked that way, pausing to watch her groom. Seamus was standing for a moment, the coffee pot held in his hand as he stared out of the kitchen window. Shandy walked up to him, finding him reaching to wrap an arm around her.

"Okay, sweetheart?" Seamus kissed her temple.

"I am. I am worried though that this step will make it worse for us." Shandy leaned against him, desperately trying to find that comfort that her Abba Father would give her.

"It will get worse." Seamus had to agree with that. "But we'll get through it. We have support here. God will protect us."

"But we won't necessarily like what we'll go through." Shandy reached for their plates, setting them on the table and then taking her mug of coffee. She sat, finding Seamus reaching for her hand.

"Seamus? Have you been receiving anything?" Shandy was troubled. The messages that she was receiving on her work phone were getting more and more vicious.

"I have been, just on my work phone." Seamus stared down at his plate. "I want this over, Shandy, but I don't know how to do that."

"We need to be out and about. Hiding isn't solving anything." Shandy pushed away her plate, her meal only partially eaten. She had lost her appetite.

"And we will be." Seamus had spoken at length with Richard and his team before the wedding, knowing that they had to make some decisions. "I transferred the paper to my office wall. We can work on it this afternoon. What about your work?"

"I am going to wind it down. I have let my clients know. I just don't have the interest in it any more." Shandy rested her chin on her folded hands, her elbows planted on the tabletop.

"No, you haven't for a while." Seamus wiped at his mouth with a paper napkin. "We're still praying through what Barnabas asked."

"We are." Shandy sighed. "I just don't know, Seamus. That's what I want to do but I'm afraid that I'll bring trouble to people."

"That's my fear." His head turned as he heard the mailbox rattle. On his feet, he headed for the front door, opening it only enough to reach into the box. He gathered the letters and headed back to the kitchen, setting the mail on the table. They would look at it later.

Silver approached her brother as he stood outside his home, reaching to hug him. They just stood in silence, Silver wanting to speak, but she didn't.

"Silver? We want to go on the offensive. How do we do that?" Seamus turned them towards the house and waited as Silver entered ahead of him. He could hear Shandy singing softly to herself somewhere.

Silver nodded. Her brother was not ready to sit back any more. She just worried too much about him.

"We can give you ideas, Seamus. It's not going to be easy,you know." Silver moved away to find Shandy, leaving Seamus staring down at the floor, his thoughts troubled.

That night, Shandy shifted on the couch, turning her head to study Seamus. He had dozed off, his head resting against hers. She was on her feet, searching through the house, checking the windows and doors. She was afraid that night, afraid that they would disappear and never been seen again.

Seamus was on his feet later, staring down at Shandy as she too slept. He sighed. How did he protect her, he wondered. There didn't seem to be a way to do that, he knew, but he would find a way. With God's help, he would do his best to protect his love.

Richard turned the next day, his thoughts troubled. He had talked with both Seamus and Shandy that morning, forwarding the nasty messages as

---

Shandy called them to himself and his team. He just didn't know where to go with them. The messages were vicious but still vague, asking for information that neither of the couple could provide.

Timothy stopped beside him, a paper in his hand.

"I found this name, Richard. We've had trouble with him. How does he factor in?" He extended the pater to his team leader.

Richard read the name, frowning harder. This name? He was an upright citizen in town, or at least that was what he appeared to be.

"Him? You're working this?"

Timothy nodded. He was as was his wife, Tate. She had refused to be left out as had the other spouses.

"We all are. We need this over, Richard. I fear for them." Timothy walked away at last, his thoughts troubled for his friends.

The man stood hidden at the back of the yard, his eyes on Seamus' house. The couple had been in and out of the house all day, just not coming to the back of the yard. That was what he needed. He needed them to come that way. Their employer was becoming more demanding, wanting the couple brought to him. They just hadn't been able to do that. They just weren't acting the way they had been expected to.

Chapter 30

Shandy walked through the yard of her house. It had been a rental and she was there to finally clear it out. She knew that Seamus was around as were his parents and many of their friends, including Jason, Bill, and Andrew and their wives. She felt content even in the face of danger. Stopping hear the back of the yard, Shandy turned to stare at her home. She had lived there for many years but was to leave it behind. She could hear the laughter wafting from the house and the yards. She smiled, a somewhat sad smile. This is when she needed her parents. Abe had called her earlier that day, asking how she was, and just letting her know that her parents were still safe and still being debriefed. At some point, she would find them. Shandy just didn't know if she wanted to.

Seamus set down the boxes that he had been carrying in the box of his truck, searching the area. He could feel someone watching them. He was afraid, he had to admit, but was trying hard to cover his feelings, not wanting anyone to pity him. He felt a hand on his shoulder as his father paused beside him.

"Seamus?" Saul didn't have to ask the question in his voice.

"We're okay, Dad, for now." Seamus' arms rested on the box wall, his head dropping to them for a moment. He felt his father's arm around him. For a moment, he felt like a toddler, needing his father's comfort.

Saul nodded. He had been through this with Silver and had prayed that Seamus would have been spared. He could sense the danger approaching.

Shandy moved further back into the yard, not seeing the men waiting there. She stopped near the back boundary, that backed onto the field and trees. She once more turned to look at the house, not seeing the men approaching her. A hand clapped across her mouth stifled her scream. She fought the arms that encircled her, picking her up and rushing through the field, leaving little evidence of where they had gone.

Bill frowned before he ran for the back yard. Something sent him that way. Andrew followed, pausing at the end of the yard, his eyes on the faint signs of a struggle in the fallen leaves. His hand reached out to stop Bill.

"They've got her." Andrew's voice held his frustration.

"They have. Right from under our eyes." Bill paced towards the field. "They were waiting for her. We can track them but I don't think we'll find them."

Seamus stopped, his eyes on his friends before they slid closed. Shandy had disappeared, of that he was certain.

"She's gone? They've got her?" Seamus felt Andrew's hand on his upper arm, turning him away from the scene and almost shoving him to the house.

His abrupt entrance startled the group who were finishing the cleaning. Looks of fear and knowledge covered their faces.

Saul was beside his son, an arm around his shoulders.

"Andrew?" Richard's voice was hard, knowledge of what had happened evident in the clipped tones.

"Shandy's disappeared. Right from under our eyes." Andrew was angry. She was in danger and they had no idea where she was. His discussion with Bill the afternoon before had shown that they had no real suspect anymore. The Whyte's could not provide any information t about who had employed them.

Seamus walked back out of the house, to stand half way down the yard, his gaze intent on the movement ahead of him. He could see the patrol offices moving around, the crime scene techs, and Bill and Jason in the midst of it all. He knew that others had stopped beside him and he could hear the prayers that were uttered. Seamus had to acknowledge once more that God was in control, that He was there with him. He turned at last, heading for the house, standing lost in the middle of the empty kitchen.

Going through the motions the rest of the day, Seamus kept looking for Shandy, not finding her. He walked back through her yard late that afternoon. The police had released the yard, leaving Seamus standing there for a moment before he moved forward. He knew that someone was beside him. He just didn't know who.

Richard's team walked with him, spreading out to do their own searching. Stephen and Naomi moved towards the field, watching carefully as they walked the path that had been taken.

"Where is she, Stephen?" Naomi's voice was quiet, showing the stress that she was under.

"I don't know, Naomi. I wish that I did." Stephen stopped at the road, eyeing the tire tracks. "It was a car that was here. Where did it go?"

Naomi nodded. She agreed with Stephen's assessment.

"We need to find her, Stephen, and soon." Naomi turned back to face the house, seeing that it really hadn't been that far. "They were waiting for her."

"For one of them. I just wish I knew why." Stephen turned as well, heading back for the house, stopping at one point to reach for an envelope. "How did they miss this?"

Naomi's eyes narrowed, her thoughts racing.

"Someone was still here, watching, waiting to leave this." She peered at the envelope. "It's addressed to Seamus."

"That it is." Stephen paced forward rapidly, his eyes on Seamus. He held out the envelope and waited for Seamus to take it.

"What's this?" Seamus took the envelope, staring at his name written on it. "Where did you find it?"

"Along the path that they took. If it had been here when the police were searching, they would have found it."

Seamus paled as he heard Stephen's words and his unspoken thoughts. Someone had still been there, waiting and watching, to leave the envelope. His hand shook for a moment as he stared at it. What would it contain? What would they ask of him? His fingers found the sealed flap before he carefully loosened it and then folded the flap back. He had no idea what the letter would say but he had to read it. All he could do was pray for his bride, his heart breaking that she had disappeared and worried about her safety.

Seamus' eyes closed for a moment before he unfolded the paper, a frown on his face as he read the words. This was not making sense, he decided.

Richard reached for the paper, his eyes on his friend before they dropped to read the letter. He too frowned. He had to agree with Seamus' unspoken thoughts. This was not from someone who wanted to harm Shandy. This was from someone who wanted to help.

"Richard?" Seamus was hopeful, that bit of hope in his voice. "Is this for real?"

"I would think that it is." Richard pointed towards their vehicles. "Come on. Let's get you out of sight and then we can work this." Richard stalked away, Seamus hesitating before he followed.

Seamus paced his house that night, his thoughts on Shandy. Where was she? Where was she, Lord? Please protect her. Bring her home and back to me.

Tears filled his eyes before he found his prayer corner, bowing before his Abba Father. He didn't move from that chair all night, rising as dawn was breaking, a peaceful look on his face and peace in his heart. God was in control. He would not allow anything to happen to her that was not in His will.

Chapter 31

Shandy fought the men holding her captive, her body twisting and turning in her efforts. Shoved into a vehicle, she lunged for the opposite door, finding her way blocked. She heard the car doors slam before the car sped off. Shandy twisted to stare behind her before a blindfold dropped over her eyes. A small scream escaped from her, despite the gruff and cruel warnings to stay silent.

She was hauled roughly from the car, her arms held in tight grips, shoved forward at a pace that made it difficult to keep on her feet. Shandy felt the difference under her feet, first pavement, then rough wood, and then tiling. Her steps stopped abruptly for.a moment before a door creaked open and she was shoved forward, the push hard enough to drive her to her hands and knees.

Shandy stayed that way for a few moments before she reached for the blindfold, pulling it off and searching the room. She was too afraid to move, too afraid to think. All she could think of was Seamus. Was it okay? Sobs shook her body as she crumpled forward. Shandy was too distraught to even think, to even pray.

Finally, Shandy rose, walking around the room, staring out of the windows. She was on the second floor, the windows nailed shut. She turned to the door, a hand resting on the knob before she withdrew it. It would be locked, she decided, locking her in and the bad men as she termed them out. Seeing bottles of water on a nearby table, Shandy reached for one, uncapping it and sipping. She sank down into a chair, her eyes on the window across from it, watching as sun sank and night drew close. Finally, Shandy's eyes closed and she slept.

The next morning, Shandy was on her feet, systematically searching the rooms, desperate to find a way out. There was no escape. Not yet. Shandy found her seat again, her eyes on the door, knowing that at some point, one of the men would be walking through the door, to pull her from it and then to a room where she might find out what was wanted of her.

The older abductor stood outside of her door, waiting, his eyes on his watch. It was almost time for Shandy to be taken to the office, to face the questions and demands. He was uneasy, not sure that she would even agree to what would be asked of her. He reached at last to unlock the door, to stand in the doorway and watch as Shandy stared back at him. He frowned. She wasn't afraid, he decided, just simply waiting for him to motion her forward.

Shandy rose at last and walked forward, trying to control her emotions and fear. She walked down the stairs, a hand on her shoulder to turn her towards the office at the back of the room. She was shoved down into a chair, the man's hand resting on her shoulder.

The man continued to frown, his mind uncertain as to the calmness that she was exhibit is. This was not normal, not in these circumstances.

Footsteps sounded on the floor behind her. Shandy waited, her heart stuttering with fear until she felt the peace and calmness that only God could and would provide in situations such as this.

"Miss Sullivan." The man's polished, nasal tones sounded as he moved to stand in front of her. "You are going to work with us."

Shandy didn't look at him, focusing on a picture of a forest in autumn behind his head. She didn't speak, didn't ask any questions. She showed no fear.

The man, Lester Whyte, brother to the two men who had been arrested, was a known businessman in town, seemingly upright and honest. He was in fact a known money launderer who had high connections in the crime scene. He needed new blood, as he put it, to move more and more money. He had decided that Shandy was just the person to do that.

Shandy worked to keep her breathing even. She was afraid, she had to admit, more afraid than she had been. This was someone whom she had met before, someone in their financial community. Had he been on the wrong side of the law all the time?

Not responding, Shandy continued to stare at the picture. She would not agree to anything that he asked. Seamus' face appeared in her vision, his with a look of complete confidence in her, the image from that morning. She could only beg God to protect her, and protect her He would.

Finally, Whyte's hand flickered and Shandy was drawn to her feet, her arm in a tight, rough grip as she was walked from the office and up to the room. The door lock clicked behind her. Shandy spun, not sure what had just happened, other than that she had been threatened in a non-verbal way. She sank into the chair, her face covered with her hands before she felt a hand touch her head with no one in the room with her. Shandy felt the peace from God flowing through her. He was there. An angel was with her. That provided protection for her.

Day by day, she was drawn from the room, to sit and wait for Whyte to appear in the office. The same questions and threats were directed at her. She just didn't speak, just didn't look at him. That puzzled Whyte. People in this situation? They were always afraid of him, always agreed readily with his demands. She just wasn't doing that.

Whyte paced his office after she was taken away that last day, a frown on his face, making it ugly looking. He needed to find a way to make her cooperate and he didn't know how to do that. Then, he spun, heading for his men, giving a quick command. Seamus would be brought to the house. Threatening him would make her cooperate, of that he was sure. Only, his men could not find Seamus in any of his normal haunts. He had been moved and hidden, Bill knowing that he would be taken to make Shandy cooperate with her kidnappers. That was what the word on the street was saying.

Shandy paced the room that night, fear rising within her. She had lost count of the days, her whole focus on staying calm and not showing the fear that was growing within her. She feared for Seamus, begging God to protect him. She didn't care if she didn't survive. Shandy just wanted Seamus to.

A sound at the door in the middle of the night had Shandy on her feet, a hand to her throat. She watched with fear as the door slid open and a man appeared, She ran towards him, recognizing Timothy. His finger to his lips kept her silent even as he reached for her hand and pulled her from the room, stopping to lock the room once more.

They fled down the stairs, their steps light and silent despite their speed. Timothy headed for the back door, fleeing through it, two more figures appearing beside them. Shandy hit the seat in a black truck, the driver not waiting until the doors were fully closed before driving off. She stared in wonder as she saw Stephen behind the wheel, Richard in the front seat, and Naomi beside her.

"How?" All she could do was stutter out that one word.

"Someone got word to Ev at her diner and she got word to us." Ev ran a well-known diner in town but was also aunt to Andrew. Richard turned to watch her before his eyes were searching the area that they were driving through. "Seamus is safe."

Shandy drew in a shaking breath. That had been her constant prayer, that her groom was safe.

"Where are we heading?" Shandy recognized the downtown area as Stephen drove rapidly through it.

"My place. Bill or Jason will meet us there." Richard was out of the truck, heading for his home, Shandy between the other three as they followed him, almost on a run.

Chapter 32

Seamus turned as he heard the back door opening and closing and then multiple footsteps on the kitchen floor. He was not turned completely around before a body hit him, his arms encircling that person, a hand on his back keeping him his feet. Seamus stared down at the lady in his arms before a sob was drawn from his body. Shandy!! Where had she appeared from?

Richard watched the couple before he turned, knowing that Raleigh would have prepared for Shandy to clean up and also prepared a meal for them. His home felt full, his team and their spouses as well as Saul and Meg milling around.

Saul approached him, Silver tight to her father. He simply hugged Richard before he stood back, unashamed of the tears on his face.

"Richard? How? Where?" Saul turned slightly to stare towards the living room, hearing Seamus' voice before he sensed them moving away, following Raleigh.

"We can't say much yet, Saul. We were told where she was and went in. Bill was watching us and had the search warrants he needed. He let us go ahead as we've had more experience in this than his team had. We cleared it with the judge." Richard rubbed at his cheek, seeing Bill appearing in the hallway. "Bill? Shandy's getting cleaned up. We'll give you our statements."

Bill nodded, heading for Richard's home office. This was going to take time. He had had word that Whyte had disappeared, out of town on business. He doubted that was the case. Whyte would have gone underground in town, his money buying him cover. The detectives had been investigating him and the judge had agreed to freeze his assets. The team had found his overseas accounts as well. He didn't have anyone he could turn to now. That made it much more dangerous for both Shandy and Seamus.

Shandy stood for a moment in the office, her hair still wet from her shower. She faced Bill, who stood, silently watching her, a look of compassion on his face.

"Shandy? Have a seat. Tell me what happened." Bill found his seat again, his notepad out to take his notes.

"I don't know what to say, Bill. This is what happened." Shandy gave her statement, a puzzled look on her face. "He just asked me to work with him. Told me that I was." She blinked, fatigue hitting her harder and harder.

"That's what we thought." Bill looked down at his notes and then at Shandy. "Go and find Seamus, Shandy. Get some sleep." He smiled at her, compassion once more on his face.

Shandy stood, staggered for a moment before she walked away, finding Seamus waiting for her. He simply wrapped her into his arms, a prayer whispered in her ear before he swept her into his arms and headed for the bedroom he had been using. He tucked her under the covers and laid down beside her, wrapping her tightly to him. He slept as well, knowing that they would be safe for the night.

Bill walked away, fatigue drawing at him. He had had enough of friends being threatened and in danger. He had no idea how to stop it but he trusted that God would protect this couple. His hand rested on the top of his car door as he looked up at the bright stars twinkling overhead before he was driving away.

Saul stood on the front porch, not saying anything. Meg was wrapped tight to him. They were still in shock to some degree that Shandy was home. But they were too much of a realist not to understand that the couple were still in grave danger.

"Saul?" Meg hugged her husband, her thoughts tumbling over what they had been told. "Whyte?"

"Yeah, Whyte. I need to find him." Saul's anger was coming through. His family was being threatened more and more.

"No, you don't. I don't want to lose you, and that's exactly what would happen."

Saul finally nodded. He knew that. He could not fight Whyte on his own.

"There has to be a way to find him." Saul looked over to where Silver had appeared, Sorley beside her. "What are your thoughts, Silver?"

"I agree with Mom, Dad. If you go out and find him, you won't survive. Right. now? He's following us, all of us. I've seen his men in the shadow." Silver looked back towards the door. "Richard and Raleigh are fine with us here tonight but I know Seamus. He'll go home tomorrow. Shandy will go back to work." Silver blinked back tears. "I am just so afraid that we'll lose him."

Sorley wrapped her in his arms. A thought cleared in his mind. He began to speak, his eyes on Richard and the rest of his team as they stood around them, Richard nodding. Sorley had come up with a plan that just might work.

The next morning, Seamus and Shandy quietly left the house, well before dawn had broken. They moved through their home, conversation quiet. They were making plans, plans that they didn't tell anyone. Some of those plans including going on the offensive, something that they knew would be highly dangerous. They found their prayer corner, sitting quietly before their Abba Father, their minds bringing forth all the verses on protection and peace that they could remember.

Shandy turned that afternoon, the mail in her hand. She dropped it on the office desk, a pen moving the envelopes. She paused, staring at the white envelope with her name printed on it. There was no address for her, just her name. No return address. Shandy felt Seamus' arm around her.

"What's this?" Seamus bent forward slightly to study the writing. It was familiar. He just couldn't put a name to it.

"This? It was with the mail. Someone dropped it here." Shandy was in the desk chair, searing the outside security feed. "The only person who came here today was the postman. Was he given it?"

"He must have been." Seamus bent forward to study the video closer. "That's not our regular guy."

"No, it's not." Shandy tapped her mouth with a slim, tanned forefinger. "How do we find out who he is?"

Seamus was in the desk chair, saving the photo from the feed and then sending it on to Emma and Bill. Emma had been quiet over the last few days, he thought, and then decided she was involved in something urgent.

"Has Abe said anything about my parents?" Shandy's voice was quiet and sounded small, not her usual vibrant tone.

"No, he hasn't, sweetheart." Seamus wrapped her into a hug, drawing her down to his knee. "We can call him later and ask." He could only pray for his lady.

Chapter 33

The next day, Abe stood in Seamus' kitchen, eying the couple. He had appeared not that long before, a friend and the lead detective from Riverville, Frankie Brennan, with him.

"Abe? What are you saying?" Shandy stood in front of him, her hands clasped together.

"That your parents will be returning here in the next few days." He watched with compassion as various emotions crossed her face. There were answers to questions that she needed to hear. Unfortunately, they would not be able to answer all of them. Some of their statements would need to stay quiet until the abductors were found and arrested. And there were abductors. Her parents had been kept from her, Brendan and Rebekah devastated at what they had been told of what Shandy was now facing.

Shandy drew in a deep breath. She wanted to see her parents, to hear what they had to say. She just wasn't sure that she wanted to hear that.

Frankie had been watching her closely. He shared a look with Abe and then Seamus.

"Shandy?" He waited for her to look at him. "They were held against their will. That much we know. Why? That's something we're working through but it does come back to this town. How much was it know that you wanted to be a financial analyst?"

Shandy frowned at him. That was a question she had not expected to be asked.

"I don't know that it was. I wasn't sure what I wanted to when I entered college." She blew out a breath, pacing around the kitchen. "I just sort of fell into it. And now I regret that."

Frankie nodded. It was not the first time that he had heard something like this.

"It's okay, Shandy. It's not the first time I've heard something like this. We'll make sure that you're as safe as you can be." Frankie had had a long talk with Bill, both men understanding that at some point, Seamus and Shandy might need to go into protective care. And they both knew they would be fought on that.

Shandy nodded, walking away from the men. The last few weeks, including the abduction, had taken its toll on her. She sank down on the side of the bed before she lay down. Sleep claimed her. Seamus came looking for her later, dropping a kiss to her cheek and then covering her with a blanket. He stood, his gaze fixed on the light sage wall across from him, a hard look in his eyes. Enough was enough, he decided. They needed to find Whyte and whoever else it was that was behind him. He knew enough of Whyte to know that he would not be working on his own.

Seamus walked through his house late that afternoon. Shandy was still asleep and he would not awaken her, not unless it was necessary. He sank into his desk chair, a deep sigh drawn from him. His head was buried in his hands for a few moments as he quietened himself before his Heavenly Father. His gaze rose at last, landing on the computer monitor. A hand reached for the keyboard and he signed in,

———

163

beginning to document his feelings about the position that he had been offered by The Barnabas Foundation. He was growing excited about the possibilities and the changes that would come to his company.

Rising at last, Seamus reached to close all the curtains in the house and turn on low lights. Standing in the kitchen, he sighed once more, and reached for bread and sandwich fixings. He turned as he felt a hand on his back, wrapping Shandy into his arms. He felt the shudders of fear running through her.

"Sweetheart?" Seamus finally spoke as he dropped a kiss on her forehead.

"I'm scared, Seamus. Really scared. I don't know that I want to meet with Mom and Dad but I need to hear what happened to them." Shandy hugged her groom. "Is there any way that we can hear what happened to them before I see them?"

Seamus nodded. That had been his question to Abe and Frankie. They agreed that would happen. Shandy needed that to understand more fully what was facing her. Somehow, what had happened to them involved her. Someone was stalking her and had been since she was a teenager. They were on the track of that person but the identity was hidden deeply under layers of companies and fake identities.

"You will. Frankie was speaking with Bill about that. They are working through the information that is available to them. It's a deep investigation, Frankie said."

"Of course it is. It always is. How do we do this?" Shandy moved to help finish off their meal, setting the plates on the table and then reaching for the soup ladle to dish up the vegetable soup that Seamus had warmed.

Reaching for her hand, Seamus bowed his head. For a moment, he was unable to speak. A sense of deep fear and terror surged through him, and his hand tightened on hers.

"We need to make some plans. Silver was around earlier, when you were sleeping. She left some information for us, plans she said." He grinned at Shandy as she shook her head. "We'll take a look at what is there, make our own plans, and then walk forward hand in hand. We just need to remember that God has already walked ahead of us and is walking right beside us now."

"I have lots of plans." Shandy grinned suddenly. "Whoever this is? They won't win. We won't let them." She was on her feet, heading for the office for pads of paper and pens. She sat once more, her eyes on Seamus, seeing his confidence in her, but also the fear that they both felt.

"We'll get there, love. I just don't understand why you." Seamus reached for the pen. "Let's see what we can come up with." He reached to kiss her, a hand lingering on her cheek. "We start doing what newlyweds do. We go for walks, shopping, out for meals. I would like to take you out for a meal tomorrow, to Ev's. We should be safe there."

Shandy nodded. They should be. Fear was growing in her heart, fear not for herself but for

Seamus and his family. She remembered the words that had lashed at her, threats against them all.

"He wants to kill you, Seamus." Shandy drew in a deep, shaky breath. "And I don't know why. I don't know that it's related to me." She frowned before she was running for the office, returning with his year books. "We went to school with his son and his daughter. I think somehow they're involved."

Seamus stared at her in shock, before he reached for one of the year books. They searched, finding the son and daughter. A finger rested on a page as Shandy looked up.

"I think that they were ones who were into drugs and crime. They set others up, to cover for what they were doing." Shandy was adamant that she was correct.

"There were always rumours about them." Seamus had to agree. His phone was out as a text message sounded. He read the message and then looked up at Shandy, a grin on his face. "Emma's has those names. She's finding information and will send it on when she's confirmed it."

"This is it, isn't it, Seamus?" She moved to hug him, feeling safe in his arms. "We're in so much danger."

"We are, sweetheart. I don't want to lose you or to see you hurt more than you have been." Seamus began to pray, knowing that their lives would be forfeit if they fell into Whyte's hands again.

———

Whyte stood in the shadows of the trees, his eyes on the house. Hatred covered his face. He blamed the couple for his family being arrested. His hand crumpled the paper that he held. For some reason, his employees were disappearing. He didn't know if they had left town or had been arrested.

He turned at last, the paper dropping from his hand, heading for his car and his home, desperate to have that drink he felt he really needed. His son and daughter were waiting for him, ready to make plans, plans that involved the death of Shandy and Seamus and their family.

A man followed Whyte, his feet seeming not to touch the ground. That man stood outside of Whyte's home, a house that no one seemed to know that he owned. He stared down at the paper that he held before he walked away, to drop the paper in Bill's mailbox before he walked away.

Bill turned his head slightly from where he sat in his living room, Cora in his arms. He shrugged, not sure if he had really heard something. He would seek that answer in the morning.

—

Chapter 34

The next morning, Seamus moved through his work building, just putting in time. He sorted through the equipment that he needed for his winter work of snow clearing. A sound behind him had him spinning, a hand clenching into a fist. He relaxed.

"Adam?" Seamus reached to shake a friend's hand. "What are you doing here?"

"Just wanted to make sure that you were okay." Adam walked through the building, his head nodding. Seamus' building was neat and tidy and well organized, just what he expected to find. He returned to stand near his friend, eyes studying him and seeing the subtle signs of fear and stress. He and his wife had been through what they all termed as an adventure.

"We're okay, I think. This is hard." Seamus rubbed at the back of his neck.

"It is hard. I remember only too well what it was like." Adam looked around again. "You're all ready for the winter?"

"I am, I think. Who knows how hard the coming winter will be." Seamus eyed his friend. "You're here for another reason other than that?" He grinned at him.

"I am. You know that I am a carpenter. I come across low income and disabled clients who need lawn care work. They don't know who to turn to. Have you ever considered anything like that?"

Seamus looked up. This was a confirmation of what he and Shandy were praying through, It had to be God who brought Adam here and with that suggestion.

"That's something that I have been thinking about lately. We're praying through expansion in that." Seamus didn't say anything more. Their prayers were confirming that they would likely take the offer from The Barnabas Foundation.

"I would like to work with you on that." Adam turned his head to study Seamus. He could see the changes that showed on Seamus' face.

"I would too." Seamus hesitated. "You know, there are a lot of people like that out there. Would Candace and Jonah come on board?" Candace ran a business providing meals to seniors and others in need. Jonah had an organic farm.

Adam stared at his friend, shock and surprise on his face. Then he nodded.

"You know, there is a whole avenue of assistance that we can look into. We'll need to meet at some point." Adam walked away at last, his mind whirling with the conversation that had just concluded.

Seamus walked back towards the house, knowing that Shandy was deep in her work. He paused before he entered the house, finding a seat on the back deck. His head bowed as he began to pray and then just sit in silence until he felt the peace that only God could give settle in his heart.

A hand on his shoulder had him wrapping an arm around Shandy, drawing her down beside him and tight to him. They sat in silence until Shandy finally shifted to look at him.

"Seamus? Something has changed?" Shandy's voice was quiet but held the confidence that she was right.

"It has. Adam was around." Seamus went on to explain what Adam had suggested.

Shandy thought it through and then nodded. That was the conclusion that she had been coming to during her own prayers.

"I think that is what we need to do." Shandy leaned harder against him. "We need to get through what we are facing."

"And we will get there." Seamus was on his feet, his hand pulling Shandy up. "We're going out for a meal. We're not hiding any more. We're newlyweds and I want to be seen out and about with my beautiful bride." He kissed her before tucking her into his truck.

Ev watched the couple as they found a seat in a booth near the back of the diner. She smiled. They had always been a couple, she decided, even from their youth. She approached them and sat across from them.

"Seamus. Shandy." Ev didn't say anything more.

"Ev? Avery around?" Seamus grinned at her. Avery was Ev's son and a federal officer, also cousin to Andrew.

"He is. You're safe here for a meal." Ev rose at last, heading for the kitchen and finding Avery standing in the doorway watching. "They're okay for now."

Avery nodded, before he looked down at the letter that he held. He would need to find Andrew that night. He walked away from the diner to do just that.

Andrew looked up as Avery sat in front of his desk and then sat back.

"Avery? You're here." Andrew sighed as he reached for the letter. "What is this?"

"About Seamus and Shandy. It just appeared on the counter late this afternoon. It was addressed to me but it should go to the investigators." Avery drew in a deep breath. "This goes a lot deeper than we thought."

Andrew read through the letter, having to agree with his cousin. He looked up and then reached for his phone, asking Bill to come to his office. Bill appeared, a question on his face before he took the letter offered to him.

Bill read through the letter many times, understanding that whoever the author of it had been, they had provided information that would help move the investigation forward. He was on his feet, heading for his office, finding Jason waiting for him.

"Jason?" Bill found his jacket, dropping the letter on the desk.

"Bill? I just got word that Whyte is waiting outside of Ev's diner. I've sent in officers but we need to be there." The two men almost ran for Bill's car, heading for the diner.

They walked towards the officer, frowning as they saw Whyte in custody. Jason headed inside to find Seamus and Shandy. Bill stopped in front of Whyte.

Whyte looked up, his wrists cuffed behind him. An arrogant look sat on his face.

"This isn't over. They will work for my organization." He was shoved into a patrol car and taken away.

Bill stared after him, worry in his mind. Whyte was correct. Given the letter that he had just been given, this was much deeper than they thought. It involved Shandy's family as well. How did they investigate this and bring it to a quick resolution? That was the question.

Chapter 35

Seamus watched the activity outside of the diner, his arm around his bride. Shandy leaned slightly forward to watch as well, her eyes turning to Jason as he sat across from them, taking with thanks the mug of coffee set in front of him.

"Jason?" Seamus' voice finally broke into the silence between them.

"Whyte. He was waiting for you two." Jason sipped at his coffee, sorting through what he needed to tell them. Bill would be in soon, he knew.

"There's more." Shandy was confident in her words.

"There is. Bill needs to talk with you. He'll be in shortly." Jason watched the area around him, feeling them being watched. He couldn't pinpoint, however, just who it was.

Bill headed in the kitchen door, finding Avery waiting for him. They stepped back outside.

"You're here helping today." Bill knew that Avery would help in his mother's diner when he could.

"I was. That's why that letter was left today. Someone has been watching all of us." Avery drew in a deep breath. "This goes deep, Bill, and goes back a lot of years.:

Bill nodded. That had been the investigators' thoughts as well.

"It goes back to when Shandy was a child, more than likely. And it draws in Seamus. We don't have a good sense of why." Bill walked into the diner, sliding on the seat beside Jason, his eyes closing for a moment. He was tired, physically tired and also emotionally tired. Too many of his friends had been through danger.

"Bill?" Seamus finally spoke. He was not about to allow Bill to ignore him and Shandy. "What can you tell us?"

"Not a lot. Whyte has been arrested. But it is not over for you. He was not the head one. He worked for someone. And it goes back years. Shandy, we have received information that this goes back to when you were young. Seamus, we're still trying to understand how you or your family has been involved."

Seamus stared at him, his mouth opening and then snapping closed. Of course, he thought, he was involved or else his family was involved. He would need to talk to his parents once more.

"What about Shandy's parents?" Seamus finally asked the question that had been dancing in the air around them, unspoken until then.

"Her parents? They're back here in town. We'll arrange for Shandy to meet with them at some point over the next week or so. This with Whyte? This letter? We need to question them on this as well." Bill and Jason rose at last, not content that they had solved anything.

Shandy watched them walk away, then looked down at the meal that she hadn't finished. She picked up her fork and then set it back down. She leaned against Seamus, seeing the turmoil in his face.

"Seamus? What do we do? We have to stay safe. But how do we keep the people around us safe?"

Seamus shrugged. That was a question that they were struggling with. Richard, Abe, and Don had all provided suggestions. It was just that none of them knew if any of the suggestions or protection offered would be sufficient and in time.

Avery slid onto the seat across from them, a concerned look on his face. Andrew followed him.

"Seamus? Shandy?" Andrew's voice was quiet but held the concern that he felt.

"Andrew? What do we do? You've been through this with so many friends, and also with yourself." Seamus looked up at his friend.

"You continue as you are. You are out and about. You can't hide. They have proven that they will come directly onto your property to get to you." Andrew looked at the couple, seeing the understanding of his words on their faces.

"We get that, Andrew. But how do we do that and keep ourselves and our families safe?" Shandy rubbed at crumbs on the table, unable to stop her restless movements.

"That is not going to be totally possible." Avery spoke up. "Whoever it is? They are monitoring your activities, where you are, who you see, what your families are doing. Shandy? Your parents are being watched as well even though they are in protective custody."

Shandy nodded, sorrow on her face. She wanted to see her parents, to hear why they had not been around her for the last few years.

"I want to see them. I need to hear from them what has happened." Shandy's voice was barely audible, broken and tear-filled. Seamus wrapped an arm around her, tucking her tight to his body.

"And you will." Andrew stood and walked away for a moment, his phone out. "Bill? Where do we stand with Shandy's parents?"

"We're ready to have them meet." Bill turned from watching Whyte being booked. "Why?"

"We need to do that and soon. She needs to hear what they have to say. This has a direct implication of what they are facing." Andrew returned to his seat, his eyes watchful but compassionate.

"Andrew?" Seamus didn't ask the question that burned on the tip of his tongue. He couldn't.

"Bill will be in touch with you. We'll get you and your parents together soon, Shandy. You need to hear their story. It's not pretty." Andrew drew in a deep breath.

"We didn't expect it to be." Shandy shifted on the bench seat. "I just need to hear them, to hear their voices, to know if they still care for me."

"They do still care for you, Shandy." Andrew's voice was quiet. "They have expressed that repeatedly and also their concern for you and your safety. They are aware that you and Seamus have married."

Chapter 36

Seamus watched Shandy that evening as she paced through the house. She could not settle down to anything, he knew. He walked towards her, stopping her in her walk. Shandy looked up at him. He simply reached to kiss her.

"I love you, Shandy. I am so afraid that I'll lose you." Seamus tightened his hold on her.

"I love you too. How do we do this, Seamus? How do we find them?" Shandy's hand went down on his chest. She heard his heartbeat, steady and strong. "I am so afraid for you, for your family, for my parents. For our friends."

"I know, sweetheart. I know." Seamus turned them towards the living room and then down on the couch. "We're in God's hands, sweetheart. He is in control. He will protect us. We may not like what we are going through, but He is there with us."

Shandy nodded, her thoughts tumbling over and over. She looked up at Seamus, finding him sitting with his eyes closed.

"Seamus?" Shandy's voice cut through Seamus' thoughts.

"Shandy?" Seamus sighed. "I know. We're in danger, we're newly married, and life should be fun. It's not." He bit at his lip for a moment. "That offer from the Foundation?"

"I know. We're still praying through that." Shandy looked around. "We're going to do that, aren't we? I don't want to work as I have been. There has to be more to life than what we've been doing. This is an opportunity for a real ministry."

"There is. I think we can let Barnabas know." Seamus didn't move. That could be done later. "Shandy? Are you ready to meet your parents once more?"

Shandy had to think through that. Her prayer over the years had been for understanding of what had happened to them. She had felt rejected by them, not knowing that they had been kept from her. Shandy had really thought that she had been abandoned.

"I think so. I need answers that only they can give." Shandy yawned before her eyes closed and she slept.

Seamus shifted how he was sitting, reaching for a blanket to cover his bride. His face was sober, his thoughts even more so. He had no idea what they were facing, other than danger. And that he wanted to remove from his bride, but couldn't.

Bill slid his paperwork into a folder and set it to one side. He stretched and then rose, walking through the department. He headed home, stopping as he stood on his front porch, reaching for the envelope hanging out of the mailbox. Bill sighed as he read it. This would be dealt with tomorrow. Perhaps this information would be enough to solve this mystery with Seamus and Shandy.

The next morning, Richard and Silver stood on Seamus' front porch, staring at the broken door. Richard walked quickly through the house, seeing the destruction and damage that had been done. He returned to the outside, shaking his head at Silver. The couple were not there.

Standing by Richard's truck an hour later, Silver could only pray for her brother, worrying more than she should be. Richard stood beside her, his phone out as he sent out text messages to his team and then Don and Abe. Those two men would be around later that day, he knew. His team would work through what they could even as they were training the team in that week.

Bill looked up as a patrol officer stopped in his doorway.

"Bill? Seamus and Shandy are missing. Richard called it in."

Bill stared at him in shock and then horror, rising to reach for his jacket and then almost run for his car. This was expected but he had prayed that it would not happen.

Silver turned as she heard Bill's car, a shuttered look on her face. She was in work mode, Bill could tell, despite her fear for her brother.

"Silver? Richard? Talk to me." Bill stood beside them, listening to what Richard had found. He nodded before he walked towards the house, seeing the traffic as it slowed in passing. He frowned. There was one car that kept passing by. A quiet word to a patrol officer had that officer moving for his car and following. He pulled it over and then made the arrest.

The driver was an employee of Whyte, one who they had been looking for.

Walking through the house, Bill studied the damage. He could only pray and hope that the couple were still alive and unharmed. But it was more than likely one of them was injured. The evidence indicated that. He stood beside Sid for a moment, watching as he collected evidence.

"Sid? Talk to me."

Sid nodded, stepping back and sealing an evidence bag before he tagged it.

"One of them is injured, Bill. I would suggest Seamus but it could be Shandy." Sid looked around. "Here. Talk a look at this." He handed Bill the evidence bag.

Bill took it, his eyes on Sid for a moment. He then looked down at the bag, frowning.

"What's this?" Bill had a good idea but he wanted confirmation.

"A tie tac. Whoever was here? They were well dressed, likely to convince them he was legitimate. He lost this in the struggle." Sid watched Bill closely. "They are getting desperate Bill. We need to find Seamus and Shandy before they disappear for good."

Bill nodded, handing back the evidence bag. He turned and walked back through the house, fear in his heart for a moment. They needed to find Seamus and Shandy but they had no idea where they were.

Silver turned as she heard another car and walked towards her parents.

“Dad? Mom?” Her voice had a question.

“We were to meet Seamus and Shandy for breakfast. They didn’t show.” Saul looked past her. “They’ve disappeared?”

“They have. We don’t know when.” Silver wrapped her arms around her waist.

“That’s what we were afraid of.” Meg hugged her daughter and then stood with her arm around her. “Where are they? And was either one of them hurt?”

Chapter 37

Saul trudged towards his house two days later, his heart heavy and hurting. There had been no sign of either Seamus or Shandy. He had gone to the streets, seeking any answers. There had been none. The people there had watched with compassion and then scattered to search for the couple. There was just no sign of them. Even the rumours that usually ran through the underground there were quiet. It was as if the couple just didn't exist.

Meg turned from the stove where she had been preparing a meal and walked into Saul's arms. They clung to one another, tears on their faces, prayers on their lips. They just couldn't do this any more, they decided, but they had no answer as to where to turn for help.

Richard studied Silver closely that day as she worked through the training course with the new team. She was struggling, he could tell, worry about her brother. He turned as he heard footsteps stopping beside him before he turned and walked from the training building.

Abe and Don walked with him. They had appeared to help and just to be there for their friend. Their teams were searching, scattering through the town, desperate to find the couple but knowing that they likely wouldn't find them.

"Richard?" Don, a lifelong friend of Richard's, finally broke the silence, his hands resting on the table they were seated at.

Richard shook his head, looking around. He was at a loss to know where to turn or where to search.

"We're working it as we did for all of us." Richard rubbed at his cheek, watching his friends nodding. "We're just not finding anything." He looked around as he heard footsteps and Bill appeared. "Bill?"

Bill reached to pull back a chair, sitting. He was on his own time that day, just appearing as a friend. It was difficult at times for him to separate work and leisure, but he did the best he could.

"How's Silver?" His words were quiet, breaking through the silence that had settled.

"She's hurting." Richard looked down, clasping his hands behind his hands behind his neck for a moment. He could hear the soft sounds of others moving around the building. "We need to find Seamus and Shandy."

"We do." Abe slid a paper across the table, unfolding it before he did so. "Take a look at this. Emma's come up with some addresses. You know your town, as do Don and Bill."

Richard kept his eyes on Abe as he silently reached for the white paper. He looked down, frowning as he read it. He finally nodded.

"Emma has been busy. These addresses? They all link to Whyte. Samuel, our friend who does title searches, has come up with these as well." Richard tapped the paper. "I know that there are people watching these. They'll let us know if there are any signs of the couple."

An hour later, Saul reached for his front door, opening it to stare at the couple standing there. He blinked and they were still there.

"Brendan. Rebekah. Come in." He stood back as Shandy's parents entered, not sure on their welcome. "It has been far too long."

Meg had appeared, surprise on her face before she reached to hug the couple. Standing back beside Saul, she studied the couple. Time and life had been hard on them. She could see it in their faces.

"Thank you, Saul. Meg. It has been too long." Brendan's voice was hesitant. "I understand that Shandy and Seamus are married."

"They are. Come. Into the kitchen." Saul pointed towards that room. "What can we get you?"

Mugs of coffee sat in front of the two couples, an uncomfortable silence in the room. Saul sighed and then simply bowed his head to pray. Brendan followed as did the two ladies. Their heads stayed bowed for a while after the last prayer before Brendan spoke.

"We need to tell our story but we need to do that to Shandy first." Brendan's voice held sorrow.

"You do. You're here now. That's sufficient for us." Meg was nodding at Saul's words.

The couple finally left, leaving Saul and Meg staring after them and then at one another.

"They wanted something, Saul." Meg was sure of her feelings.

"They did. I just don't know, Meg. I need to know the circumstances around their disappearance before I can fully trust them again. There's an undercurrent there that never was before." Saul reached to wrap his wife in his arms. "We need to pray over this and pray for our kids to come home." He felt Meg nod before he felt sobs shaking her body.

Silver stood and watched her parents before she climbed the steps towards them, her walk slow and heavy. Saul reached to include his daughter in his hug.

"Dad? What happened?" Silver finally walked away from him to pace the porch. Something had, of that she was certain.

"Brendan and Rebekah were here. There's something odd about what happened to them." Meg answered. "We need to investigate that. Silver, you can help."

Silver nodded. That was the conclusion that her team had arrived at. Abe and Don were in agreement with that.

"That's why I'm here. We're meeting tomorrow at the building. We want you two there." She looked towards the road. "We don't want to include Shandy's parents as yet."

Saul nodded, watching as dusk slowly dropped down. He was afraid, he decided, more afraid than even he had been with Silver. He turned at last, hearing the conversation between Silver and Meg. He paused, looking up, feeling the presence of God in a way that he had never felt before.

187

Shandy paced the room that she was locked into. She had searched the room over and over, looking for a way to escape, a way to get away. There was none. She worried about Seamus. They had been separated as they were pulled from their home. Shandy had pleaded to be kept with him, knowing that he had been injured. She had been refused, shoved into a truck, and driven away. She couldn't tell if Seamus was in a vehicle behind her or now.

Turning away from a window, Shandy stared at the door. There had been no contact with whoever it was that had taken them captive. She had fully expected. That added to her fear. Shandy knew full well that was the plan, to drive her to fear and make her cooperate with her abductor.

A sound at a window had Shandy spinning that way before she cautiously approached it. A hand covered her mouth to still her scream. She turned for a moment to study the door before she was back at the window. The man waiting there put a finger to his mouth before he disappeared. A few minutes later, Shandy was standing outside of the locked door, watching as the man locked it once more before reaching for her hand. She ran towards the street, disappearing into the building across the road. The man listened as he heard a car slow and then stop before he ran with Shandy towards the back of the building and then through more buildings before Shandy had to admit that she was lost.

Shoving Shandy into a room, the man slammed the door shut and locked it, standing in front of it to prevent Shandy from accessing it. He stood, arms crossed over his chest, his eyes on her. His face was stern but his eyes compassionate. The group he worked for had been looking for the couple. A chance overheard conversation had led them to Shandy. Their leader didn't feel that they could wait, needing to remove Shandy that day and then hiding her away.

"Who are you?" Shandy's voice quivered as her fear rose with in her. When the man didn't answer and just kept watching her, she turned and began to systematically search the room. The only windows were too high for her to reach. The only exit door was behind the man. Opening a door, Shandy stared at the small, neat and clean two-piece bathroom. This was well planned, she decided, before she found a seat in a clean and comfortable arm chair. Her eyes closed as she began to pray and then slept, her body unable to handle any more stress.

The man, Joseph by name, nodded. It was what he had expected. He pulled out his phone and read the text message that had just arrived. A few quick taps of his fingers sent the response that Shandy was safe. They needed to hide her until they could retrieve Seamus. And that was a question they needed to answer. Seamus had not been kept in the same building as Shandy. With her disappearance, it became that much more dangerous for him.

His team spread out, two of the men watching that building, as others searched through paperwork and on the street. They were on a timeline that if they missed it could well mean the death of Seamus. That they needed to prevent at all costs.

Bill turned as a youth from the street approached him, simply slipping him into a dirty piece of paper before he was running on, making it seem as if he had only stopped to ask a question.

Bill took a quick glance at the paper and then headed back to the office. He sat in his desk chair, the paper flat on the desk top. He sighed. Shandy was safe, he was told, just not where. But there was no evidence or answer to where Seamus was being held. He feared for Seamus. Bill needed to find Seamus and find him fast.

Andrew found Bill later that day, just sitting quietly in front of his desk. He just waited for Bill to finish his phone call and the notes that he needed to make before he looked over at Andrew.

"Bill? Talk to me."

Bill handed over the evidence bag with the note. Andrew read it and then nodded.

"Shandy is safe. That we can confirm?" Andrew looked up, his eyes keen.

"We can't. A youth from the street passed it on to me and then was gone before I could ask any questions. I won't find him now." Bill was frustrated at that.

Andrew nodded, quickly understanding the implications.

"We need to find Seamus. How is that going?"

Bill sighed even as he shook his head. There had been no sign of him in the building, from what the note said. That meant the couple had been separated. The race was on now to find him.

Andrew looked around, taking in the stack of files on Bill's desk. All of the detectives had heavy case loads and that they could not figure out why.

"Bill? What are your thoughts? Have you looked into the owner of the building?"

"I have, Andrew. It traces back to numbered companies, a huge layer of them. Carrie's working through that but she's running into road blocks. She's reaching out to Samuel." Bill sat back, his pen tapping at the desk chair.

"That's good. Keep me in the loop." Andrew was on his feet, walking through the building and then heading for his own office. All he could do at present was pray for his friends, that they would be home soon and safe.

Shandy woke, her eyes staying closed as she heard soft sounds and conversation around her. Her hand felt the material under her hand and remembered being freed. Only it didn't seem as if she was free, just under the care or control of other men. Shandy didn't know if she could trust them or not. On her feet, she faced them, Timothy turning as she rose.

Joseph walked towards her, his head tilting to study her.

"Shandy? Go on and get cleaned up as best you can. Sara brought in some clean clothes for you. I'm sorry that you can't have a shower or bath. This is the best that we can do." He walked towards the door, followed by the two other men, leaving an older woman standing near Shandy.

"I'm Sara. Go on. Joseph is correct. We've brought you some supplies and clothes." She smiled with compassion as Shandy's eyes closed and she was unable to control her tears. "We're looking for Seamus. We'll find him. We need to debrief you."

Shandy nodded, turning to the washroom, locking the door behind her. A hand touched the clothes waiting for her as well as clean towels and bottles of soap and shampoo. She looked up, a simply prayer of thanks offered.

Chapter 39

Joseph watched Shandy closely as she sat, a bowl of soup in front of her before he found the chair across from her. She glared at him from under her brow, bringing a small smile to his face.

"You are safe, Shandy. We are actively searching for Seamus. For now, we'll keep you here. No one other than out team knows where you are." Joseph reached for a folder before he paused. Shandy had pushed away her bowl, her hand reaching for her mug and wrapping her fingers around it. He nodded to himself as she didn't respond. Joseph opened the folder and then simply slid it across the table. "Read this. Then we'll talk."

Shandy didn't take her eyes away from him even as her hand landed on the folder. She drew in a deep breath before her eyes dropped. She read, page by page, turning each one to lie face down. She looked up at last, not quite understanding what she had read,

"What is this? What does this mean?" Shandy's winced as her voice sounded almost too loud in the room.

"This? This is what your parents have been up to. They were recruited by a security company, sent in under cover to live with this crime family. They put their lives on the line to do so. They had to cut all ties with you, couldn't contact you at any time. We have had someone watching them for years, just in order to ensure that they are safe. Abe, a friend, went in and brought them to safety. They are here in town, as you know." Joseph's voice hesitated. "They do need to meet with you but for now, until we bring down the group that they were with, they need to stay hidden and safe." He sighed. "Although they did go and see Seamus' parents."

"They did? After we disappeared?" Shandy's eyes slid closed, tears trickling down her face before she swiped at them.

"It was. They didn't stay long and we have no idea what was said. This has put Saul and Meg in danger. Richard has moved in and has them safe." Joseph was on his feet, his phone out as he studied a text message that had come through.

Sara sat beside Shandy. This rescue was something that they had done many times in the past and she felt it getting old. She wanted to retired and settle down. Elmton suited her just fine.

"Shandy, we need to keep you hidden. I know that you want to be out there, searching for your parents but more importantly searching for Seamus. We can't have you doing that. That would put you and anyone around you at risk." She looked around. "We'll find something for you to do."

Shandy looked around the room, seeing the comfort that had been provided. She saw a door that she had not seen before.

"What's behind that door?"

"A bedroom, Shandy. Somewhere you can sleep without fear. Whoever is after you has to get through us first." Sara was on her feet, reaching to refill the mugs with fresh coffee. "Talk to me about your work. We've been watching you, just because of your parents. I don't think that you are happy."

Shandy stared at her before her head shook once more.

"No, I'm not. I want to do something that helps people more than just analyzing someone else's portfolio. I mean. I make money but that's not what I want." Shandy didn't think that she had explained herself very well.

"That is you." Sara agreed. "Now, what do you do about it?"

Shandy shrugged, her thoughts turning to Seamus. Where was he? She needed him with her, only he wasn't.

Sara looked up as the door opened and Joseph returned, He sat, his eyes on the folder that lay in front of him. He sighed as he looked at Sara, who frowned and then nodded.

"Joseph?" Shandy's voice was quiet but it held a myriad of questions. "What aren't you telling me?"

"There's not a lot that we can tell you, Shandy. You understand that this is a full-blown investigation and has been for a number of years. Your parents? They willingly went undercover for us. It hurt to walk away from you. They are praying for you to understand. Once we can get you together with them, they will explain. For now, we have to keep you and them undercover and with full security." He paused. "Our leader has spoken with Richard, Don, and Abe.

They are aware of the situation and are ready to move in if we need them to."

Shandy nodded before she rose and paced, turning at last to the bedroom. The door clicked quietly behind her before she threw herself across the bed, tears overcoming her and fear for her groom uppermost in her mind. She could not pray, but knew that her Abba Father heard every word.

Joseph had turned his head to watch her before he turned back to Sara. He sighed once more.

"How do we do this, Sara? She'll want to be out there and looking for him." Joseph rubbed at his neck.

"She will be. We need to involve her in the investigation. She'll dig into it. She knows her town." Sara just waited, knowing that Joseph would think it through and then discuss it with their leader, Ben.

"Yeah. We need to do that." Joseph leaned back, his body sagging slightly from fatigue. "She does know her town. And we'll likely need to bring in his parents and sister."

"At some time, we will." Sara was on her feet, her eyes on the clock. "We'll eat, Joseph, and then go through the paperwork. You have new information."

Joseph watched Sara as she worked, something that she had done many times in the past. He knew that she was ready to retired and had chosen Elmton to do that. He would miss her. She had insights that others on the team didn't have.

"Sara? What are your thoughts? I know that we've gone over it many times but you've always held back something." Joseph was on his feet to refill his coffee mug.

Sara paused in her motions, her thoughts tumbling over and over. She nodded.

"We do need to talk, Joseph, but I want Shandy to be there. This affects her in a way that Ben isn't even aware of." Sara said nothing more, just walked to the bedroom door, tapped on it and then entered when she heard Shandy's voice.

Chapter 40

The next day, Shandy took the thick folder that Sara was shoving at her, sitting back in the comfortable chair. Joseph silently handed her a pen and high-lighters and walked back to where he had been sitting. He watched her closely, praying for her and for her to understand what she had been handed. Ben was on his way, knowing that he needed to be there. He had had a long talk with Sara and Joseph the night before, finally understanding just how deep this went. He had then reached out to Andrew, meeting him at Ev's diner. Two hours had passed before Andrew had reason, a folder in his hands.

Shandy read through the material and then read more slowly, her pen and high-lighter working. Finally she sat back, staring at the floor, her mind whirling at the confirmed information. Looking up at last, she found Sara watching her closely. Shandy jumped slightly as she saw an older man sitting across from her, someone she had not heard coming in.

"Who are you?" Shandy's voice wavered slightly.

"I am Ben." He smiled at her. "I know your parents, Shandy. We were friends during school. I want this over for all of you and to bring your groom back to you."

"You can do that?" Shandy's voice was even quieter, not sure that she could trust the man sitting in front of her.

"We can. We have your parents here in town. They are in protective custody, Shandy. We'll get you to them soon. This adventure that you're involved in? It won't last much longer." Ben nodded at Sara who moved to sit near Shandy. "We have found Seamus. We'll be moving in soon to free him."

Shandy stared at him, her mouth opening and closing, hope rising in her eyes and on her face. Had God heard them? She felt free suddenly, free of the watching eyes, the shadows that had followed her everywhere, the fear of what was coming next, of disappearing and not being found ever.

"Thank you. What can I do?" Shandy was ready to go on the offensive, ready to find her groom and bring him home.

Ben nodded slowly. Shandy was at the point that they had all known she would reach, just sooner than they had expected.

"All right then, Shandy." Ben leaned forward, his elbows resting on his knees. "This is where we go and what we have planned."

Shandy listened carefully, her eyes not moving from Ben's face. She heard soft movement around her, not realizing that the full team had arrived, a team of eight. They were stern and sober, their thoughts on Seamus and how they would need to work it to bring him home.

Looking around at last, Shandy stared in shock at all the people with her. The room felt crowded and then she sighed. This is it, isn't it?

"What do we do now?" Shandy refused to back down from Ben, seeing the slight smile on his face.

"We finalize our plans. Those plans include you staying here for now." Ben's hand rose. "We need to keep you hidden, They are searching for you, Shandy. You will not survive if they find you. We have received word from the street that they have put a hit out on you. They mean to kill you." Ben's voice was gruff. He feared for the daughter of his friends. He had watched her over the years, especially since her parents had gone undercover. That had disturbed him but they had know they had to break contact with her to keep her safe. Even then, Shandy had been watched. That had increased in the last few months, leading Ben and his team and the other authorities involved fear for Shandy's life. Seamus had become involved just because he was good friends with Shandy. Or at least, that was the rumour. They had not been able to confirm or deny that.

"I don't understand. I need to do that." Shandy refused to back down from him. "You say you know my parents. How?"

"Your father and I were friends since we were in Grade one. Your mother as well. I left town after college and rarely came back. I couldn't. Not with my work." Ben stared around the room, gathering his thoughts. "Shandy, your parents were approached to go undercover in a company. Part of the condition was that they could not tell you. They had to walk away. Leaving like that almost broke their hearts. They wanted to tell you but didn't dare. All they could do was ask that someone watch out for you. There has been someone here in town all these years doing just that." Ben could say no more. It had to remain secret.

Shandy rose and walked away. She needed to take time to absorb what she had been told. To hear that her parents had gone undercover like that? It had never crossed her mind that they had done this. Shandy had always thought that they just walked away from her.

Ben had risen as Shandy left, a concerned look flickering across his face. They needed to end this investigation and end it soon. He walked away himself, leaving his team working on the end pieces of the investigation and then walked into the police department and asked for Andrew.

Andrew stood in the shadows of the hall for a short time, studying Ben before he walked forward, bringing him back to his office, beckoning for Bill to follow them. Bill frowned as he did just that, not sure who this older man was.

"Andrew?" Ben spoke quietly. "We have Shandy. She's safe." He saw the look of relief that crossed Andrew's face and then Bill's. "We have a line on where Seamus is but we can't confirm it."

Andrew nodded, watching Bill for a moment, knowing that he was struggling with trying to comprehend and understand what was being said.

"Bill? You've talked with Shandy's parents. Ben here is a friend of theirs. He has been aware all these years of why they went undercover and who asked them to. He has had someone watching Shandy.

Unfortunately, they had been unable to prevent what has happened to her or Seamus."

"I don't understand." Bill was at a loss, listening carefully to Ben's words. His face grew stern as he realized the implications and danger of what was being discussed.

Chapter 41

The day they disappeared, Seamus had fought to reach Shandy, constrained from doing so. He felt the blows that landed on his body, blocking the pain as he struggled to escape. He didn't feel the slash of the knife across his abdomen, adrenalin blocking the shock and pain. Seamus was dragged from his home, watching as Shandy was shoved into a vehicle. He was shoved roughly into a truck, hitting the back seat before he reached for the opposite door, desperate to escape and find his bride. He was roughly pulled backwards, his hands bound in front of him.

His head twisting and turning, Seamus sought to find the other vehicle, the one that carried his bride. He didn't see it. He slumped back against the seat, his eyes turning to the men with him. There were four. Three had been the ones who had invaded his home, breaking through the door as Seamus and Shandy had looked through their kitchen to decide what they wanted for a meal. Seamus drew in a deep breath, still not feeling the pain from the stab wound. He had tried so hard to protect his lady but hadn't been able to.

Hauled roughly from the truck, Seamus stumbled as his feet landed on the rough ground. Shoved forward, he walked towards the building and through the door. Shoved forward once more, he landed in an interior room. There were no windows, only a light bulb hanging from a high ceiling. He staggered for a moment, a hand to his abdomen, not realizing that he was bleeding from a wound that needed attention and that wouldn't get it. Seamus searched the room at last, a hand on the wall that helped keep him on his feet. The only other door was one to a small washroom.

Despairing, Seamus turned in a circle once more, finally sinking down on the narrow bunk. He was trapped, he decided, trapped with only one way out. And that way was locked. He hadn't tried the door but he knew that it would be. He looked up for a moment, before he began to pray, not for himself but for his bride, seeking comfort and peace that only God could give.

His body giving in to pain at last, Seamus collapsed back on the bunk, a hand resting on the wound, his other arm flung across his face. He slept, his body twitching from pain.

The door opened slowly and an older man entered, bent from the years. He stopped beside the bunk, setting down the supplies that he had in his hand. He reached to move Seamus' hand from his abdomen, carefully moving the T-shirt up on his body. The man shook his head. This had been unnecessary, he decided. Seamus had likely been controlled. This was done just as a vicious attack, an attempt to take Seamus' life.

Seamus stirred briefly, pain crossing his face. His head was lifted carefully and he was forced to drink, swallowing the pain medications that had been placed in his mouth. He was needed alive but the man wasn't sure that he would live. The wound was deep in some place, well beyond what he could treat.

Gathering his supplies, the man walked back to the door, pausing to turn and watch Seamus for a moment. He shook his head before he walked out of the room, the man waiting in the hallway locking the door behind him.

Seamus didn't rouse the next day or the day after that. His wound began to show the infection that his body was fighting. The man tried his best to clean it and dress it once he was done. It just wasn't working. He stood on that last day, his eyes on Seamus before he turned to the door. At the moment, he was the only one in the house. Turning back to Seamus, he drew him to his feet, an arm around his waist, Seamus' arm around his shoulders. He stopped to lock the door behind him before he walked Seamus from the house and to his rackety old car. Seamus slumped in the passenger seat, his eyes closed, pain evident on his face.

The man drove away, knowing that he had likely written his own death warrant but he had to help. He heard the words that had been uttered loudly by the man who had employed him. Seamus would die, one way or another, and his body hidden away where no one would ever find it. He couldn't allow that to happen.

The car showed before it turned into a narrow driveway, the rougher terrain causing Seamus to groan. Stopping, the man sat for a moment, staring at the house in front of him before he was out of the car and around at the door to draw Seamus gently from the car and guiding him towards the small log cabin that sat in front of them. He tapped at the door and then opened it, surprising the younger man who rose from where he had been sitting at a table, a book open in front of him, a mug of tea sitting at his elbow.

"Dad?" Jeff Walker stared at his father and then at the man his father was holding upright. He was across the room, helping Seamus to stay upright. "What's going on?"

"He's been hurt, son." Jase Walker nodded towards the spare bedroom. "Let's get him onto that bed. He needs your help, son."

Jeff stared at his father for a moment before he was walking Seamus towards the room. Jase was ahead of him, drawing back the blankets and then moving to find the supplies that his son would need. Jeff was a surgeon, working at the local hospital.

"Dad? What's going on?" Jeff worked away, assessing Seamus even as his eyes lifted briefly to father's face.

"He's was kidnapped, son. They hurt him." Jase sighed. "You know what I do. You know that this is the last time I am working undercover. I had to get him out of there. They were planning on letting him die and then just dumping his body somewhere it would never been found. His family doesn't deserve that."

"We have a fight on our hands, Dad." Jeff rose at last from where he had been bent over the bed. "I need to get some supplies and medications. You're safe here." He was away, the cabin door locked behind him before he moved his father's car into the detached garage, hiding it. Driving off, he watched carefully for anyone who didn't belong but didn't see anyone. He breathed a thank you to God, knowing that the Great Physician would be the One who would heal Seamus. He could only do so much.

Seamus fought the fever that wracked his body, the pain from the wound driving him deeper and deeper into darkness. Jeff despaired of saving him until a day came that Seamus no longer tossed with fever or pain. He slept, Jeff standing beside his bed, reaching to adjust the IV that dripped lifesaving fluid into his body.

"He'll make it, Dad." Jeff looked up at his father, seeing his father nod. "We need to find someone to speak with."

Jase sighed. He knew that. He would head for town, to find Jason or Bill. He just worried that he would be found and followed, bringing danger to his son and Seamus.

Chapter 42

Seamus stirred slowly, his eyes opening. He stared around, a frown covering his face. His head turned on the pillow as he stared around. He didn't recognize the room. Trying to sit up, Seamus' body just would not cooperate with his wishes. He slumped back against the pillow, not hearing the soft footsteps that approached him.

Jumping, Seamus stared up in fear at the older man bending over him, lifting his head to help his sip from a glass of cool water. A hand rested on his forehead for a moment.

"You're safe, Seamus." Jase watched him, seeing the moment that Seamus understood and then slept. "We'll keep you safe and get you back to your lady."

Jase asked out of the bedroom, pausing for a moment. Jeff turned and watched his father.

"Dad? How is he?" Jeff waited for his father to speak.

"He's been awake." Jase rubbed at his cheek. "I spoke with Bill again yesterday. He'll want to come out and get his statement."

"He will need to. Likely tomorrow." Jeff reached for a pot and dumped in a container of broth. "I'll heat this and see how much I can get down him."

"We can do that. Listen, son, I'll head in and find Bill." Jase walked away, leaving Jeff to stand in the cabin doorway and watch his father. He prayed for his young companion, knowing that God was healing him. It was up to God to bring this adventure or whatever it was that Seamus was involved in.

Seamus was awake again later that day, able to push himself up on the pillows stacked behind him. He looked around the room once more, before his thoughts turned to Shandy. He began to grieve, sure that she was dead. He tried to pray, to beg God for His protection. His thoughts turned to the promises of God. Seamus looked up at last as the door opened and Jeff appeared. He frowned at the man.

"Jeff? Is this your place?" Seamus' voice was shaky.

"It is, Seamus. Dad found you and brought you here. You've been sick. The stab wound is healing at last." Jeff handed Seamus a glass of water. "Here. Drink this. Tomorrow, Bill will be out to speak with you. Don't say anything to either Dad or I."

Seamus nodded, turning his head to stare at the window. He was afraid to ask, to ask if Jeff knew if Shandy was safe.

The next morning, Bill tapped at Jeff's door, waiting for Jase to open it. Jeff was at the hospital, reluctantly leaving his father. He sensed the danger approaching them and worried, before he had to turn his worries to his Heavenly Father.

"Bill? Come on in." Jase closed the door behind Bill. "Let me help Seamus out here for you. The coffee's hot." He walked away, heading to where

Seamus had finally been able to clean up. Doing that had drained his strength.

Jase studied Seamus for a moment before his hand was around the younger man's arm, helping him to his feet and then to a seat in the living room. Bill watched his friend closely, seeing the damage that had been done to him. He shook his head. When did it all end for his friends?

"Bill?" Seamus drew in a deep breath. "You need to know what happened. I don't remember anything, or not much. I can remember fighting to get to Shandy and then to get out of the truck they shoved me into. I remember a room with no windows and then nothing. I can't describe the men or the truck."

Bill nodded, knowing that was all that he would get from Seamus. He looked through his notes, his thoughts troubled. There was something that they were missing, something crucial, and he had no idea what it was or who it was. And until their team discovered that or someone came forward, then they were at a standstill.

Seamus rubbed at his face, his eyes closing. He was fatigued, both in body and spirit. His emotional well seemed dry. He felt as if he had been abandoned by everyone, including God. He just didn't feel that presence any more. Seamus knew that wasn't true. God was there, protecting him, covering him in the hollow with His hand, hiding him in the cleft of the rock.

"Bill? Shandy? Is she okay or even alive?" Seamus' voice was broken and barely audible.

Bill studied his friend, knowing that they needed to get Seamus and Shandy together again. That would happen in the next day or so, he prayed.

"She's fine, Seamus." He gave a small smile of understanding and compassion as Seamus' eyes slid shut. "She was rescued a couple of days ago and is being kept hidden."

On his feet, Bill moved towards Jeff.

"Jeff? How is he?" Bill turned to watch Seamus as he sat, his head bowed.

"He's healing. Seamus was in trough shape when Dad brought him here." Jeff bit at his lip. He couldn't say much more than that. He couldn't say how Jase had found Seamus or where. That wasn't his place.

Bill gave him a keen look before he nodded. Jeff knew more than he was saying, Bill knew, but he didn't press. Sometimes, he had to let things slide for the moment. It usually came out in the end.

"Tell your dad thanks for us." Bill walked away at last, his steps hesitating as he paused before Seamus, praying for his friends.

Andrew turned in the break room as he heard footsteps stopping behind him. He nodded before he poured mugs of coffee for himself and Bill and then pointed towards the hallway. Neither man spoke until they were in Andrew's office and with the door closed.

"Bill?" Andrew waited for Bill to speak. He was only too aware of how dangerous it had become for both Seamus and Shandy.

"I spoke with Seamus." Bill watched as Andrew thought through that before nodding. "He's healing from a stab wound to the abdomen." He went on to describe his talk with Seamus and then Jeff. "Jeff knows more than he's saying, and I think it goes back to his father." He was frustrated however. "We need that one piece of information."

"We do, and it's just not coming." Andrew sat back, his face thoughtful. "You're not hearing anything from the streets. You would have said if you do. That tells me either they don't know, they're scared, or they're protecting you or Seamus or Shandy."

"That's what I think." Bill stood, frustration on his face. "I have to set this aside for now and I don't want to." He walked away, his mind already turning to other investigations.

Chapter 43

Shandy stared at the paperwork being shoved across the table towards her. She looked up at Ben who was smiling quietly at her.

"What's this?" Shandy poked at it, not reaching for it, not reading it.

"More information." Ben's grin grew wider as he heard Joseph and Sara laughing beside them. "I know. That's all we are giving you. This?" He tapped the papers. "This may just solve it."

"I see." Shandy finally reached for it, her eyes dropping. She began to pray, begging God for closure, for ending of this adventure, and to be be reunited with Seamus. Her thoughts were troubled and sober as she pondered what God was teaching her through all this. Shandy had to admit that she was learning to trust more, to reach out in faith that God was in control and wanted only the best for her.

Her thoughts continued to be troubled as she read through the stack of papers, her pen marking certain statements and writing her own questions. She sat back at last, her hands clasped on the table in front of her,, not saying anything. Shandy looked up at last, finding Ben watching her, a compassionate look in his eyes before he bowed his head and prayed for her and for Seamus. Her own eyes closed against her tears. She refused to let them fall.

Shandy finally spoke, her words concise even though the three with her could hear the trouble and worry in her tense voice.

"I know who it is." Shandy looked up, her eyes blinking with her emotions. "God help me, I know who it is." She uttered a name, not looking at Ben or the other two. She didn't see the quick look of surprise or comprehension that crossed their faces. 'Where do we go from here to prove it?" She finally looked at Ben before she reached for her phone, sending a text to Bill.

Bill reached for his phone, grumbling at the number of text messages and voice mails that had been coming through all that day. He stopped as he read the message from Shandy, his eyebrows rising in surprise before he read it over and over. On his feet, Bill searched for Jason.

"Jason? Got a moment?" Bill hesitated in Jason's doorway, looking behind him for a moment. He entered the office, closing the door behind him before he sat. He stared at the text message still open on his phone before he handed it over to his fellow detective.

Jason took it, watching Bill for a moment. He sensed the frustration and concern that was coming through. Glancing down at the message, Jason stared at it.

"Is this for real? We're sure it's from Shandy?" Jason handed Bill back his phone.

"It is. She knows her community." Bill sat back as he tucked his phone away. "How do we prove this?

He's very prominent in the community, especially the financial community." His head tipped back for a moment as he stared up at the ceiling. "And he supports the police board."

"Good way to keep track of everything. How deep does it go?" Jason's mind was racing, trying to determine just how far the corruption would find its way into their force.

"That we don't know." Bill stared back at Jason. "What do you have on your desk?"

Jason studied the folders on his desk, mentally reviewing where he stood in each investigation.

"A lot of them I'm waiting for information. There are three or four that I am actively working." Jason looked back at Bill. "You want me on this?"

"I do. I'm asking for Sid to come and help you. Keep it between the two of you. If you need to work at home, do that." Bill was on hsi feet, heading for the lab supervisor to make his request. That woman simply nodded and turned to find Sid.

Sid walked into Jason's office and sat. He had no idea why Bill had made the request that he did but there was a reason. He stared at Jason as he explained what they would be doing and nodded.

"Where do we work?" Sid was on his feet once more, following Jason as he headed for his car and then followed Jason to his home.

Jason's wife, Maria, turned as she heard the two men, not surprised to see them.

"What can I do?" Maria greeted Jason and then Sid.

"Keep the coffee pot on. We'll be putting in long hours." Jason headed for his home office, Sid on his heels.

Seamus was on his feet, still somewhat unsteady, but pacing. His thoughts were troubled. He turned as he heard Jase stopping near him.

"Jase? Thank you. Where do we go from here?" Seamus didn't move, just stood, his hands rubbing together before he shoved them into the pockets of the sweatshirt that he wore. He wanted to go home, to find his bride, and just shut out the world.

"We find Shandy." Jase nodded, a small smile on his face. "Yes, we will find her today. We need to put the two of you together."

Seamus' eyes slid closed. They would be together but it was still dangerous. He could feel the danger growing around them, He felt as if he was being sucked into the eye of a tornado, the storm whirling and building around them.

"Today?" His knees buckled with shock and then he sat, his eyes back on Jase. "She's okay?"

"Tonight. We move in after dark." Jase sat. "There are some rules that we need to follow, Seamus. Before you ask, your parents are safe. Silver is as well. I've talked to Richard and his team. They are ready to move in to help if they need to. So are Don and Abe." He leaned forward, his elbows resting on his knees. "It is going to be dangerous to get you to where we need you. We have set up protection for you both. That means keeping you both hidden until Bill and his team are ready to move it. They are working hard on this. There's information that Emma is forwarding to us all. We'll let you see it tomorrow. For now? Get some rest. You won't over the next few days." Jase rose, walking away to open the door and walk outside. His walk took him around the yard and the house, searching for any sign that Seamus had been found. The man that he had rescued him from was brutal, not afraid to kill anyone who got in his way, not matter who they were.

Chapter 44

Shandy stared down at the clothes in her hands before she glared at Sara, who grinned at her. She had no idea why she had been given that outfit, including a wig.

"What is this?" Shandy glared at the clothes and then at Sara again. She could hear a laugh from Timothy, who stood behind her.

"It's to change your appearance, Shandy. Today? Today we move you. And to do that, we need to change your looks. Go on. Get changed. We're leaving in fifteen minutes." Sara's hand shoved Shandy gently towards the bedroom, watching as she stalked that way and shut the door behind her.

"She's ready to fight." Joseph's quiet comment broke the silence in the room.

"She is. This is when she'll run." Sara sighed. "And we will be running right after her. That would be quite the line of people trailing after her."

Joseph laughed again, picturing that. He turned as he heard the door to the room open and Ben appeared. That man peered around, looking for Shandy.

"Everything ready?" Joseph asked, his eyes on Shandy as she came back into the room. She was unrecognizable, dressed in tattered clothes and a rainbow coloured wig. She frowned at the three watching her, seeing the grins on their faces. She looked up. Lord, we need your protection right now.

This is where it gets dangerous, isn't it? You are the only One who can bring us through this. Please protect my Seamus. I love him so much but am so afraid of what will happen in the next while.

Ben nodded. Shandy was ready, he could see, ready to stand and fight.

"Okay, Shandy. Let's get you out of here. We have work to do and that means we need to connect you with Seamus." Ben pointed towards the door. He walked that way, Sara following him.

Shandy hesitated for a moment before she walked that way as well, Joseph following her, locking the door behind them. She sat in the back seat of a car with darkened windows, watching as the streets of her town flashed by. Shandy frowned as she saw where they were heading. Her eyes closed. They were heading for Richard's place.

Joseph stopped the car, not turning it off. Ben was out of it and into the office building, hunting for Richard.

Richard turned as he heard footsteps, a hand out to shake that of Ben's.

"Ben? You're here?" Richard walked towards the reception area of the building.

"I am. We have Shandy outside. Where's Seamus?" Ben didn't wait for Richard to reply before he was pacing the room.

"He's in my house. Don moved in with his men and is helping to keep him safe. They're good to stay for the next week." Richard turned as he heard footsteps. His own team had appeared, having been waiting for Ben to arrive. "Okay, team. We've made our plans. Time to put them into play." He walked away, heading for his house, Silver and Timothy with him, Stephen and Naomi heading out of the building with Ben.

Joseph and Sara drew Shandy from the car. They could feel eyes on them and prayed that they could get Shandy inside before she was hurt. Stephen and Naomi walked with them. Shandy focused totally on the house, desperate to get inside and out of the sight of whoever was out of there. She stepped inside Richard's house, taking a deep breath and feeling safe once more.

Searching the home, Shandy's socked feet whispered across the wooden floors. She was searching for Seamus, knowing that he was there. She had been told that but more than the words that had been spoken, she could feel him. Shandy finally found him in the sun room as he stood, staring out of the French doors, his hands tucked into his jeans pocket. She stood, a hand covering her mouth to still her sobs, tears on her face. He was here, he was alive, and all she had to do was walk across the room to be enfolded in his arms.

Seamus stirred, some small sound bringing him back from his thoughts. He stared at the window, seeing an image there, an image of a beloved lady. He rubbed at his eyes, certain that he was seeing things, that his wishes were making it seem that she was there. A small sound had Seamus turning, just in time to catch Shandy as she threw herself at him. He staggered for a moment, pain wafting through his body as hers hit him. Her sobs shook him, drawing his own tears.

An hour later, Shandy sat on the loveseat in that room, tight in Seamus' arm. The outfit and wig had been discarded. He just refused to let go of her, despite the discomfort he felt. Their eyes were on Bill as he sat nearby, his attention on the folders that he was reading through. He had not said anything when he arrived but his grim face had said it all.

Whyte's employer stood across the street, hidden in the trees, watching the activity around the house and buildings. He was angry, a hand striking at a nearby tree. He needed the couple to come to him. That wasn't happening. He could feel the forces moving in on him, the ropes closing tighter and tighter. He walked away at last, heading for his office and the plans that he was trying to make. He was beginning to fear the oncoming waves of justice creeping closer and closer to him.

Standing near the road, Stephen's phone was out as he took a photo of the car. They had been watching it for the last few hours and knew exactly where the man had been standing. They had taken turns crossing the road and moving quietly behind him. He sent the photo to Bill and Sid and then to his team and Emma. Emma had been quiet, he realized, not sending on the information that she usually did. He wondered at that before he shrugged.

Bill looked up at last, his gaze centring on the couple across from him. His eyes locked with Sid's for a moment before he looked past him to where others were waiting. Saul and Meg were there. He sighed. This is when it would become more dangerous for all of them. Bill knew that Brendan and Rebekah had been moved to a more secure building, hiding them from anyone who might find them.

"Bill?" Seamus finally spoke, his words hesitant, his voice not his usual confident one. "Can we spend time in prayer?"

Chapter 45

Seamus stood at last, watching Shandy as she slept. He took the blanket that Raleigh handed him before he walked from the room, looking for his father. Saul turned as he saw his son, wrapping him into a hug, a father prayer whispered in his ear. Standing back, his hands on his son's shoulders, Saul studied him, seeing the changes that had happened in him over the last few weeks.

"Dad? Who do you think it is?" Seamus wiped at the tears on his face. He felt broken, unwanted, and unable to continue. He felt his father's arm around his shoulders, drawing him to a seat at the kitchen table. He sensed movement around him but didn't look up.

Saul studied his son once more, knowing that Richard was there as was Sorley. Both men sat, their hearts breaking for the man in front of them, knowing that he was at the point where he either broke totally or drew from God's strength to continue on to the end.

"Who do I think it is?" Saul hesitated before he spoke. The name that came from him had the others nodding. "He's hidden in plain sight. He always has been."

Richard was nodding. He knew the man, had always been uncomfortable around him.

"I think you're right, Saul. He's been around for so many years. There have always been rumours about him." Richard reached for a pad of paper and pen. "Let's start listing what we know about him."

An hour later, Shandy's hand rested on Seamus' shoulder. His arm drew her down beside him, a kiss dropped on her temple.

"What have you guys done?" She reached for the paper, reading their notes. Her gaze lit on Sorley, watching him. "Sorley?"

"I think we have one of them but I think there is someone else. I just don't know who." He sighed. "We say that all the time. There is always one more person."

Richard nodded, even as he pulled out his phone. Emma had sent an email. He read it aloud, hearing the silence from the others.

"She's right on, I think." Sorley had finally broken the silence. "And she's pinpointed the other person. A woman. That doesn't surprise me."

"No, it doesn't." Shandy's finger traced the name that she had written down on a piece of paper. "It's her. She's related to him, a sister if I remember correctly. No, half-sister. They try and hide their relationship." She looked around at the men and then at Raleigh and Meg. "We need to make plans."

"And we will." Meg pulled back a chair beside Saul, her hand finding his. "What do we know about them and their businesses?"

Heads bent as they began to work, pens scratching on the paper in front of them. Quiet comments came quickly and then laughter. Sorley and Silver looked at one another before the suggestions began to flow about how to trap the pair. Each suggestion was more outrageous than the one before it.

Seamus sat back for a moment, studying each one with him. He realized that the rest of Richard's team and their spouses had joined them. Shandy was on her feet, working with Silver and Raleigh to prepare meals. Timothy and Stephen were in and out of the room, making their rounds outside, on guard to protect their friends. His eyes closed for a moment as he grew still before his Abba Father. God was there, he acknowledged, and protecting them. They had gone through trials but He was walking them through it. They had felt His presence, gently reminding them that they were not forgotten or unavenged.

Bill walked in at last, fatigue weighing down his steps. Jason was beside him, prepared to stay and work with the group. He looked around, took the material handed him, and then left, heading for home and his wife and children. He desperately needed to see them, to be reminded that life goes on but there is a lot of good still there.

Jason sat beside Seamus, simply waiting for that man to speak. Shandy was tucked under Seamus' arm.

"Seamus? What are you two planning?" Jason spoke, guessing that they would go on the offensive.

"We're not sitting around any more, Jason. We need to find this person and draw them out. We can't go on as we are. I want to live life with the lady I love and adore so much, and we can't." Seamus was sober, fully cognizant of what they faced. He had talked to all of their friends and also Emma. They had all been candid with what they had faced and how they had felt.

Shandy peeked around Seamus at Jason. She knew that his sister had been through a horrible adventure, one that had almost meant her disappearing from his life forever.

"Jason? We need to do this. I love Seamus so much and I don't want to lose him, not so soon." She breathed out hard. "Okay. So, starting tomorrow, we will be out and about in the town. We move back home. Seamus continues to work as he needs to, including preparing for the new year. Me? I am wrapping up my business. I am not working as a financial analyst any more. I want to branch out into something else."

Jason nodded. This is what he had expected them to do.

"We'll have people around you as much as we can." His hand went up at their protest. "You know how it works. We try our best to protect you. We can't promise that you won't be hurt again. That's out of our hands."

Seamus turned late that night. They had remained at Richard's home that night, just as it was so late. He watched as Shandy slept, tossing and turning at her troubled sleep. He finally laid down beside her and gathered her close to his heart. He was so afraid that he would lose her, begging God to keep them safe.

Shandy roused somewhat in the early morning hours. She turned in the bed, studying Seamus as he slept. Her hand rested against his cheek, seeing the lines of pain and stress that lined his face. All she could do was pray for her groom, not knowing how much danger they were still in.

Chapter 46

That morning, Seamus stood in the kitchen of their home, feeling unsafe. Someone had been in there over the days that they had been missing. He reached for Shandy's hand, pulling her out and back towards his truck. He drove off, Shandy twisting on the seat to stare behind her, her phone out to call Jason. He simply stated that they needed to find somewhere to wait, he would search their home, and would they just stay safe?

Stopping in the parking lot at Ev's diner, Seamus turned off the ignition and then just sat, staring out of the windshield. He finally reached for Shandy's hand, his grip tight and almost desperate. He bowed his head, despair in his voice as he prayed. They were not safe, not yet, and just when they would be, they had no idea.

"Seamus? Who was there?" Shandy's voice barely broke the silence in the truck cab. She didn't look at him. She stared around the area around them, seeing friends, townspeople, and strangers moving through their daily walk.

Seamus shrugged, not able to say. He dropped down from the cab and came around to reach for her, hugging her before he reached for her hand, drawing her with him into the diner and then to a booth at the back of the diner. Ev watched them, frowning for a moment. Avery stood beside her, his own eyes searching the diner. It was a quiet time for them, with few customers. He felt a chill of fear run through him.

"Avery?" Ev's voice was low as she spoke to her son.

"I know. Mom. I know. I feel it too." He looked around. "Something is about to happen." He turned and walked outside, standing for a moment. He didn't hear the footsteps that sounded lightly behind him before a heavy blow took him down. His body was dragged behind a dumpster and left bound and gagged.

The men crept back to the outside door of the kitchen, reaching to open the door. Startled kitchen staff looked around, their hands raising at the weapons that was held on them before they were herded into a storage room and the door locked behind them.

Ev frowned as she turned, hearing soft movement from the kitchen. She stepped to where she could see the kitchen and then spun, moving quickly to Seamus and Shandy.

"Quick. We need to leave." Her hand reached for Shandy, pulling her with her and out of the diner door, running for cover. Seamus followed, his head turning every few seconds to watch behind them.

"Ev?" Shandy finally slid to a stop, standing hidden in a doorway of a broken down building, breathing hard. Seamus stood in front of the two ladies.

"Someone was in the kitchen. The staff disappeared." Ev was worried about Avery. She didn't know if he was safe or not.

"They found us." Seamus pulled out his phone, calling for aid to the diner. "Where do we go?"

"I have no idea." Ev searched the area before she was running again, Seamus and Shandy following her, their path covered by people from the street who moved in and covered their flight. She reached for a door, pulling it open and then heading for a hidden room. "In here. We'll be safe." The panel clicked behind them, leaving them standing in the dimness, breathing hard, worry and fear on their faces.

Bill and Jason moved in quietly and quickly, their weapons in their hands. Other officers surrounded the diner, moving in at the same time. Calls for the men inside to put down their weapons and surrender rang through the air. The men inside spun, surprise on their faces, before they complied.

Releasing the workers, Bill listened as they asked about Avery. He spun on his foot, heading for the outdoors and searching, finding Avery still unconscious. He stood. back as he watched the paramedics work over him before heading off with him to the hospital.

"Bill? Where's Ev?" Jason was puzzled.

"Somewhere safe. She would have taken off with Seamus and Shandy, trusting that Avery would take care of himself." Bill walked over to Seamus' truck, his hands cupped around the side window to look inside.

Ev, Seamus, and Shandy walked slowly towards the diner, watching the activity around it. They stopped beside Bill and Jason, startling the two officers. Bill pointed towards Seamus' truck, sending them off with a police escort.

———

Walking through the department, Bill dropped into his desk chair for a moment. He knew that the three had given statements and had been taken to somewhere safe. Avery was on his feet, angry that he had been attacked and unable to help prevent the attack. Andrew had spoken with him before he sent him to find Ev.

Seamus couldn't sleep. His mind just wold not relax. His eyes on Shandy, he reached for her hand.

"Shandy? What do we do? That was too close today." Seamus feared for his lady love. "I love you so much. I don't want to lose you."

"I love you too, Seamus. We need to draw them out but how do we do that?" Shandy's eyes closed as she pictured the man and woman and what she knew about them. Her words began slowly and then she spoke more quickly.

Seamus stared at her and listened to her plan, a smile beginning to stretch across his face. He reached to hug her, praying for them and for those they would need to involve.

"We'll make it, sweetheart." Seamus knew that they would. He just didn't know how harmed they would be. He had been hearing more and more of the viciousness of the two.

"I know. I just worry about those around us." Shandy reached for her phone, sending out a group text with instant results. "We can't stay hidden. That only delays it. I talked to Jason after I gave my statement. They're getting ready to move in, just needing to confirm a few more details and then obtain the arrest and search warrants." Shandy yawned, her body tired but her mind too active for her to sleep.

"We'll get there, sweetheart." Seamus reached for his phone, a grin crossing his face. Silver was weighing in, refining their plan. He knew that Sorley would be involved in that.

"So tomorrow, we go back out there. We walk away from our protection and do that." Shandy reached for Seamus, knowing that they would spend their time in prayer.

Chapter 47

Shandy stood still on the sidewalk in the downtown area of Elmton. It was the next day, and she and Seamus had simply walked away from Richard's home and headed for town. She knew that there were others around them. That didn't make her feel any safer. Seamus kept her hand tight in his.

"Are we ready for this?" Seamus' voice was low, worry evident in it. He looked around as well, seeing Richard and others around them, not close enough to be noticeable but close enough to protect them.

"I don't know that we are but we have to do this." Shandy looked up at him, marvelling at his height once more. "I don't want to lose you, Seamus, but I understand that God is in control. He wants only the best for us."

"We need to remember that we were prayed for in the garden. He is here with us. He has walked this before us and is walking it with us now." Seamus tugged her into a walk. "We do need to move, sweetheart. We can't stand in one spot."

Shandy nodded, her eyes searching the area. She knew that someone was following them, someone who didn't mean them good.

The man and woman watched as the couple they were desperate to take into their custody again walked freely through the downtown area, They followed them, arguing between themselves about how to do that.

Richard and Silver exchanged a look, slight smiles on their faces. They followed them couple, close enough to almost touch them. They knew the other three on their team were there as were Don and his team. They were determined to finish it that day, to set Seamus and Shandy free from the worry and fear that had dogged them for so long.

Stopping suddenly, Shandy drew in a deep breath. She had caught a glimpse of the man in a store window, closing in on her. Seamus looked down at her, his hand tightening on hers.

"They're here?" He kept his voice low.

Shandy nodded, sensing the couple closing in on them.

"They are. They are right behind us." She drew in a deep breath as she looked up at him before she turned and faced the man and woman behind them. This was not what had been discussed or planned. "Tyler Whyte. Gerry Black. What a surprise! Or not."

Seamus stared down at her, horror on his face for a moment, swallowing hard. Shandy had just stepped outside of what they had planned. He had to trust her, of that he had no doubt. He just wished that she hadn't stepped forward like that.

"Shandy. Shandy. Shandy." Gerry Black mocked her. "Who names someone that ridiculous name?" Her tone was mocking. In her mind, they were in control. "You're coming with us."

Shandy stood her ground, simply shaking her head. She stepped backwards, Seamus moving with her.

"I don't think so. I do have to ask though. You're close to my parents' ages. Why?" Shandy's voice was calm and neutral.

"Why? Because we could. We've been involved in the underworld of this town for years. I won't say what all we've been involved in but you are now going to work for us." Tyler spoke, his voice hoarse and sounding like a heavy smoker. His eyes were bloodshot and his body showed his love of rich food and alcohol. He gave a short barking cough.

"We understand that. We just want to know why me?" Shandy studied them before she nodded. "You wanted me to tell you who my clients were, to let you know who had high bank accounts or a large investment portfolio. Then you would move in on them. Blackmailing them. Threatening them. Using them to launder your money from crime. How am I doing?" Shandy stepped backwards again, sensing someone behind her. A quick glance showed Don and his team member, Thomas.

Tyler and Gerry shared a look, a frown on their faces. How had she figured that out? They didn't think anyone could.

Seamus kept his attention on the area around them. He knew there was help nearby but he still feared that something might happen to them.

"How did you know that?" Gerry reached for Shandy, her hand claw like in appearance. Seamus pulled Shandy to one side, causing Gerry to stumble, losing her balance and drop to her knees. She screamed in rage and tried to scramble back up but she unable to rise without help. Her high heel shoes scratched at the pavement.

Tyler sneered at his half-sister, not helping her at all. He reached for Shandy himself, his hand freezing in mid-air as he saw the men standing between him and Shandy. He spun, seeing the group that had closed in around them, Bill and Jason approaching with their badges out. Tyler gave a cry of rage and spraying towards Shandy, finding himself tackled and taken down. The patrol officer clicked the handcuffs around his wrists, a little harsher than normal.

Richard nodded at Bill before the security teams had surrounded Seamus and Shandy, rushing them from the area and to safety. Bill would track them down for their statements. For now, they needed to be safe.

Silver hugged her brother later that day, holding on for a little bit longer than normal before hugging Shandy. The feeling of relief coursed through them all, bringing fatigue.

Seamus reached for Shandy after everyone had left. His parents had shown up for a while before they too left. She clung to him, shudders running through her before she looked up.

"It's over?" She didn't believe that it was.

"It is, sweetheart. It is over. We just need to do a follow up with Bill and Jason." Seamus bent to kiss her. "I love you so much. I thought that I would lose you."

Shandy kissed him back, muttering that she loved him too. And just where were they to go now? He laughed softly as he hugged her once more.

Chapter 48

Seamus stared at the man standing in his kitchen, his eyes on his face and not the weapon that was directed towards him. Shandy's hand rested on his back. He had shoved her behind him when the door had opened and the man had stalked into their home.

"What do you want?" Seamus' voice was firm but held the fury that engulfed his body.

"You. You're both coming with me." Trevor Adams stood there, a frown on his face as neither of the couple moved. "Now?" His voice barked out an order.

"No, I don't think so." Seamus folded his arms across his chest, his stance stating that he was going nowhere. He had caught a glimpse of movement outside the house and on the deck. Help, he prayed, was here. He just had to keep Adams' focus on him. "I just would like to know why."

"Why what?" Adams continued to frown at the couple, not comprehending why they were not moving and why he could not move any further towards him. He didn't understand that God had intervened, providing protection for them.

"Why us? You have to be the one employed the Whyte's. You're what, in your late 30s. What do you want with us?" Shandy peered around Seamus, anger on her face.

"Why? Sure, I'll tell you. You're not going to live to tell anyone." Adams didn't hear the slight creak of the back door as it opened and Bill and officers stepped quietly into the room nor the opening of the front door and quiet footsteps as other officers approached from that direction, standing out of sight of the room, just waiting. "Your parents, Shandy? They work for me. I have a whole network throughout this province that is mine." He tapped at his chest, proud in his words and in his life of crime. "I control the crime in this area. I'm reaching out. You will work for me, Shandy. You'll continue your work in finance and provide that to me. You will cover my crimes. Seamus? You're my insurance policy. You stay alive and safe is she works for me." He didn't hear Bill stepping closer. A cry of anger sounded from him as Bill's hand reached to grasp his wrist in a tight hold, tight enough to cause the weapon to drop and spin across the floor.

Seamus followed the path of the weapon in fascination, realizing just how close they had come. He looked up at Bill, who nodded towards the front of the house. Seamus wrapped Shandy into his arms as he stepped outside and then walked away from the house, turning to stare back at it.

"It's over, Seamus?" Shandy's voice barely broke through the still air.

Seamus watched the activity around them, the lights from the cruisers sending blue and red rays across his property. He hugged his bride tighter, bowing his head to thank God that they were safe.

Bill approached, tucking his notebook away. He stood for a moment, his face turned to the autumn sun, just taking in the fact that another friend had survived an adventure. He was getting tired of friends facing these life and death situations.

"Give us a couple of hours and you can go back in." Bill squinted at them. "It's over. We'll meet in a few days, just to update you on where we stand. It's messy."

"It is." Shandy walked away, heading for Seamus' truck ,knowing that he would want to head for his parents.

Saul and Meg hugged the couple, taking in their words that their adventure was over.

"We need to get together with everyone." Meg's words filled the room. "Saturday."

Saturday found everyone gathered at Richard's. His was the largest home and he and Raleigh had quite willingly opened it up for a celebration. Shandy walked the yards, her thoughts troubled. She wanted to meet with her parents but that had not been arranged yet. She turned as she heard footsteps on the pathway and stopped, a hand covering her mouth. Brendan and Rebekah stood here, tears on their faces. They've aged, Shandy thought, before her feet were moving and she was wrapped in hugs from her parents, hugs that were long overdue.

Brendan looked at his daughter at last, seeing the stress that she had just been through and then looked at Seamus. He moved to hug that man, a hand resting on his shoulder as he stepped back.

"We're okay, Shandy." Rebekah's voice was low and broken. "We'll work through this. We were

___

asked to go undercover and help bring down Adams. We just didn't think it would take that long." They turned back to the house, finding the others waiting for them.

Shandy sat, wrapped in Seamus' arms, her eyes finding each one gathered there. Even their pastor, Silas and his wife, Madigan, were there, ready to lead off in a time of prayer. They sat back at last, everyone watching Bill and Jason. Andrew stood near the doorway, knowing that they could only say so much.

"Okay, people." Bill's voice finally broke the silence. "This is what we can say. Adams did in fact employ the Whytes. They were his contact here. He was involved in many crimes. Shandy? He really did think that you would provide information on your clients and help set up fake accounts to cover his activities. He didn't count on your honesty. Seamus, because of your friendship with Shandy, you were targeted in an effort to make her cooperate. We know how well that worked." Laughter broke through his words. "Brendan and Rebekah? You agreed to work for an investigative team working to bring down Adams. It took a long time to do that. Those years you will never get back with Shandy. Thank you."

Bill, Jason, and Andrew walked away at last. There was still work to do but they felt a relief that for Seamus and Shandy had survived what they had been through. They had all seen their strength and faith in their Heavenly Father. He was the One who brought them through, strengthening them, protecting them, and letting their witness shine to those around them.

———

Seamus stood for a moment, plates in his hands, watching Shandy as she worked at putting away what food was left. He turned at last, the kitchen tidy, counters wiped down, He reached for Shandy, heading for their prayer corner in the living room. Sitting, he wrapped her tightly into his arms.

"Okay, sweetheart?" His voice, although low, was love-filled.

"I am, finally. Mom and Dad are back. We have work to do there but it will come." Shandy reached to kiss his cheek. "And you?"

"I am. I hate that we had to go through this but God has shown us just how powerful He is. And I have the love of my life right here in my arms." He kissed her and then rested his head against her. "We need to make plans but not tonight. Tonight we just rest."

Two months later, Seamus was on a hunt for his bride. She wasn't in her home office and didn't seem to be anywhere in the house. He reached for his jacket, shrugging into it and heading for his work building. He opened the door, hearing soft singing. Shandy was here, in his office. Seamus stood for a moment in the office doorway, leaning against the door frame, a smile lighting his face.

Shandy looked up from the paperwork that she had spread out over the desk. She was on her feet, throwing herself into her groom's arms, her face raised for his kiss.

"Happy, sweetheart?" Laughter laced Seamus' voice.

"I am. And so are you." Shandy spun away from him. "We survived and are safe. We're moving forward with our lives. We have our friends and families."

"We do." Seamus walked to the desk, studying the paperwork. "You're sure about this?"

Shandy wrapped an arm around him, her head resting against his arm.

"I am. And so are you." She touched the signed contract that they had just sighed. "Barnabas sent a text message, welcoming us to the family. I am looking forward to working with those who need my help." Shandy tilted her head to study Seamus. "And so are you."

"I am. This means that I can hire those who need work. We can help those who can't afford lawn care but can't do it themselves. God is working through us, sweetheart, just as we have prayed."

They stood for a moment before Shandy gathered the paperwork and filed it. Turning, Seamus reached for her hand, locking the building and then heading for his truck.

"We need to celebrate." Seamus paused, looking around his property before he walked around the truck. He paused to pray, his hand reaching for Shandy's. They were safe, their families and friends were safe, but they still had to face the trials. God would provide what they needed to get through that.

"Where do we go now, Seamus? We're starting a new chapter with work. But personally, what can we do to help others?" Shandy had been thinking through what they could do.

"I don't know, sweetheart. For now, we need to heal. When that happens, then we can decide what we want to do." Seamus reached for her hand as they walked towards Ev's diner. They would eat and then find their refuge, a house that Shandy had turned into more of a home that Seamus had.

Thank you for picking up the story of Seamus and Shandy. I undertook this novel as a challenge with an author friend to write 50,000 words in a month. It is the first time in months that words have flowed as freely as they did. Maybe retirement isn't so bad after all.

Seamus and Shandy? Theirs was a love story over the years. Throughout their adventure, they found the strength and protection that God provides. They may not have totally understood how much that God had been there but they knew that He was. That is Who He is - our strength, protection, Abba Father.

My prayer for you would be that whatever you face you find that strength and protection for your Abba Father. He is there all the time. He never leaves us or forsakes us.

God bless

Ronna

www.ingramcontent.com/pod-product-compliance
Lightning Source LLC
Chambersburg PA
CBHW070501300726
48975CB00007B/2269